Consuming Fire

Consuming Fire

PAULETTE LeBLANC

RESOURCE *Publications* • Eugene, Oregon

Resource Publications
An Imprint of Wipf and Stock Publishers
199 W. 8th Ave., Suite 3
Eugene, OR 97401

www.wipfandstock.com

PAPERBACK ISBN: 978–1-5326–6761–9
HARDCOVER ISBN: 978–1-5326–6762–6
EBOOK ISBN: 978–1-5326–6763–3

Manufactured in the U.S.A.   DECEMBER 15, 2018

For God, who never forgot about me

"No man knows how bad he is, till he has tried very hard to be good"

C.S. Lewis

Contents

Introduction

THE IDEA FOR THIS book came about, as most fiction does; like a thump on the head. One morning it occurred to me that sound theology played out in a story might make an interesting read. Ben Gerard is a simple man of faith. He leads a quiet life, with one prayer and one passion.

Consuming Fire takes two breaths at once, in the form of simultaneous plots. While Kaitlyn Blythe is a quick-witted orphan who assumes God has simply forgotten her, Cameron Stowe is an atheist headed for the Ivy League, who would never make such an assumption. I wanted to explore the dichotomy of the Christian faith, in showing damaged characters that experience genuine grace. Both the evolution and conviction of these characters is deeply rooted in the compassion shown them by seasoned Christians.

Ben Gerard and Pastor Bill Jeremy have been placed in the lives of these two kids with a message that they are already loved, rather then a lecture on how to behave. Ironically this ignites a spark of faith based on relationship rather than rules. Consuming Fire attempts to shine a light on the condition of the human heart, as it is both imperfect and beloved by our creator.

1

Intangibles

IN THE WHOLE SCHEME of things, Ben Gerard would have said he was right where he should be. Of course he'd have said that on any given day. He'd felt it coming for months. The weight of the situation moved toward him first like a shadow growing in his thoughts and finally like an ache planting itself in his bones. The feeling of something looming on the horizon became so intense that it was almost tangible . . . and then it was.

He squinted into the setting sun and swallowed down the rest of his coffee, praying his usual prayer about whether or not it was all right to go about God's business in this way. The door of his old truck whined its usual high-pitched squeal as he swung it open and checked his watch. He walked around the back to lower the tailgate when the radio squawked at him from his pocket.

"Ben, you out tonight?"

"Roger that Logan."

"Need help unloading?"

"Not that feeble yet," Ben said, chuckling.

"Route 45?" Logan asked.

"Is there any other place to fish?"

"I never know whether or not to wish you luck."

Ben took a deep breath and nodded.

"I know just what you mean Sheriff."

He waited for a moment, wondering if Logan was going to say anything more. He wanted to get the motorcycle unloaded before anyone passed by and saw him there. He stuffed the radio back into his pocket and rolled the bike down off of the trailer. He stood it on the dirt road and took a rag from his pocket to wipe away any dust. It was maybe the only thing he owned that he might classify as pristine. Though it rarely saw any action, it was built for thrills and speed and the young boy in him couldn't resist the excitement it stirred. He shook his head at the pure invention of it but he knew this bike in particular had been bought for a purpose, so he'd see to that. It was simply to be used as bait, a beautiful lure set out to catch a thief, or a fish, as Ben called them. He slid the key into the ignition and looked over his shoulder before he got back in his truck.

Ben hated this part. The waiting was almost intolerable. He turned to the comfort of prayer once again, asking forgiveness if he caused one to stumble in his attempt to restore what God had intended.

"Ben?"

The voice from his pocket startled him and he quickly pulled the walkie-talkie to his mouth again.

"Yeah Logan, go ahead."

"Trap set? I mean, you all set?"

Ben looked out the window and sighed.

"I'm afraid you had that right the first time, Sheriff."

"I'll be up the road in the usual place."

"I appreciate the support."

Ben nibbled a sandwich he'd brought along in his cooler, wondering how many of these they'd done now. He thought about Malachi and Billy. Then there was Johnny Niccoli. The thought of him made Ben chuckle to himself. The ones who showed up as hard as nails often made the biggest turn around. What a cliché, and yet, he knew it to be as true as his own name. It amazed him how people could spend years letting the world tie knots in them that take God no time at all to pull apart. His mind spun to Ray and he stopped eating for a moment. He looked out the window as a car slowed, did a drive-by on the bike, then kept rolling. Ben put the sandwich down and turned on the radio. Maybe he'd get some news. As he poured the coffee from his thermos, thoughts of Ray stayed with him. All the men he caught seemed like Ray to him now.

"No one's gonna grab it if you're only sitting ten feet away," Malachi said, laughing and caused Ben to jump a little.

"You made me spill my coffee Mal."

"How long you been sitting here?"

"Not long, since the sun started going down maybe."

"Logan waiting up the road?"

"Yep."

"Got enough for the weekend yet?"

"God always provides," Ben said, nodding.

"God provides criminals?" he laughed.

Ben narrowed his gaze at him.

"I'm just having fun with you," Malachi said, restraining his laughter.

"You all set in the kitchen?" Ben asked.

"Mostly. I'll call the team before the weekend and remind them about what they're supposed to bring."

Ben searched Malachi's young blue eyes as though he had much to learn.

"What is it?" Malachi asked. "You look like an old bear scoping out a salmon."

"The weekend is fast approaching. Go do your job and let me do mine."

"Okay," Malachi said, raising his brows.

"We all right?" Ben asked in his usual way.

"Yeah."

"Mal, we all right?"

"Yeah Ben, we're all right."

He watched the kid saunter off in the rearview and shook his head, smiling to himself. Ben gave him a hard time, but Malachi knew what was at stake. Ben never thought a young buck as wild as Malachi once was would end up his right hand man. In all honesty, Ben couldn't do without him, but if it wasn't Malachi, it would have been someone else God sent his way. The thought that it might have been Ray wiped the smile from his face.

* * *

Ben didn't mind living alone. If Rosie had told him he'd be this content without her, he would have argued an entire day away over it. But the truth was he didn't mind the quiet. He didn't mind having only Roofus and Caesar to keep him company. He didn't even mind having to do all the shopping and cooking. Rosie would have been proud of how domestic he'd become.

He scratched Caesar's head and plopped a can of cat food into his bowl. Roofus came sniffing around and Ben called him to his kibble. He wouldn't have to work that hard to keep Roofus away from Caesar's cat food. Caesar would let him know when he'd gone too far. He had the scars to prove it.

"Good dog," Ben said, patting Roofus's head. Caesar looked up from his bowl, licking his lips.

"I suppose you want some attention now too?"

Ben sat at the edge of his bed and took off his watch, placing it on the dresser. He kicked off his shoes and went to the bathroom to wash up. As he brushed his teeth, he stared at his reflection. He wondered how all the years of his life had settled on his face day in and day out without his say so. Strange, he thought, how no one would confuse him for a twenty, thirty, or even a forty-year-old, when it seemed like just yesterday he *was* a twenty, thirty, or forty-year-old. Sixty was an age he'd always thought of as old and far away. He didn't feel old in his brain, where it mattered, though his body definitely hadn't felt the surge of youth in a long time.

"Thank you God for all the blessings of this day. For all the change I've seen for the better in this world. Thank you for divine appointments, please don't let me miss one. Forgive me any liberties I take on your behalf, and close those doors I needn't walk through. Send any my way if I can help Lord, and keep them away if I can't. Tell my Rosie I love her, and I'll be home whenever you've finished with me."

He paused then the same way he always paused. He'd wanted so badly to pray about Ray. Even in the privacy of his bedroom, he couldn't muster up the courage.

"Please take this thorn from my side when you see fit to remove it. In the name of Jesus, amen."

* * *

The bells on the door tinkled their hello at him, as Ben pushed them open and took a seat up at the counter. In his opinion, Annie's was the best place in town for breakfast, evidenced by his three or four mornings a week there. Raquel smiled and placed a cup of coffee in front of him.

"Good morning Mr. Ben."

"Morning Rock, the usual please."

"Two over easy with crispy bacon," she yelled to the kitchen. "My nephew Cameron needs to come on one of your weekends," she said.

"Does he *want* to come?"

"Want to doesn't matter. If you'll let him, I'll make him."

"What's going on there? Remind me," Ben said, sipping the hot coffee.

"He's been driving my sister crazy since his dad died last year. He used to be an honor student, involved in all kinds of academic clubs. Everyone said it was just a phase—a part of grieving, ya know? Well, either everyone was wrong, or he isn't finished grieving yet, because now he's just a plain handful. He's got a new group of rowdy friends. He's coming in at all hours, just heading down the wrong road."

"Listen, here's what I want you to do." Ben pulled a scrap of paper from his pocket and scribbled a phone number on it. "Tell Cameron to call this number and ask for Bill Jeremy. Bill will know why."

"So you don't think he should do one of your weekends?"

"Let's catch it before it comes to that."

Raquel became distracted as she pushed Ben's paper scrap into her apron pocket. Ben followed her eyes to the tinkling doorbells behind him where a man stood with hopeful eyes and clothes that reeked.

"Sorry, nothing this morning," she said, shaking her head.

The man turned and went back out the door.

"What's that about?" Ben said, raising his eyebrows.

"He comes around every once in a while asking for work in exchange for food. If I need dishes done or the trash taken out I usually let him do it and give him something to eat out back."

Ben narrowed his eyes at her and nodded. She poked her head out the door.

"Flip," she called, and waved him back in.

Raquel looked at Ben, and he could tell from her expression that she was going to tell this man that he'd wanted to buy his breakfast. Ben shook his head sternly, wanting her to keep that to herself. He opened his newspaper and sipped his coffee.

"How do you feel about a couple of eggs and some bacon?"

"That would be most appreciated," Flip stammered. May I wash up in the bathroom first?"

"Sure, it'll take a few minutes anyhow. You can pick it up at the counter, and eat out back."

"Much obliged Ma'am."

Ben turned another page of the paper.

"Out back?" he murmured.

"If I seat him up at the counter, no one's going to want to sit here. You can smell that jacket from across the room."

Ben wasn't about to tell Raquel how to do her job but it seemed to him the man deserved the dignity of eating in the dining room.

"What about the booth in that empty corner by the men's room?"

"Ben Gerard, you are a man I could never say no to," she said smiling and shaking her head.

"As you did not do it to one of the least of these, you did not do it to me," he said under his breath.

"What's that mean?" she asked, making her way to Flip's table with a cup of coffee.

"Just that one day we'll all see one another a little more clearly, Rock."

* * *

Ben rolled the bike down the ramp, gave it a quick wipe, and then stood it in the dirt. Taking Malachi's suggestion, he pulled way down the road this time. He didn't like being this far away but he supposed it would be all right, as long as Sheriff Will was just up the road in the usual spot. Ben hadn't heard from him, so he scooped up the radio.

"Logan? You out here?"

Ben gave him a minute to respond.

"Will?"

Before the thought that he should wait on Logan could finish making its way through Ben's mind, he saw his pristine motorcycle tearing up the dirt road and coming straight at him.

"Jesus, be with us both," he said, hitting the ignition and spinning the truck to follow.

"Logan, Logan, pick up. Fish on the line, I repeat, fish on the line."

"Ben?"

"You get lost on your way out to Route 45 tonight Sheriff?"

"Got caught at a traffic stop just before—what's your location Ben?"

"Still on 45, coming up on the Grove Street Bridge."

"Identification?"

"Negative. He's wearing a helmet."

"You got yourself a safety concerned bike thief," said Logan.

"Seems that way."

"I'm coming around the back of the bridge now. I should meet up with you both in the middle."

6

Though his motorcycle was being taken, Ben still marveled at the machine. As its rider pulled on to the bridge and under the wood cover, the engine whined even louder. Ben couldn't help but feel exhilaration in the moment for which he'd almost felt guilty, however the thought of excitement had danger on its tail. They'd never had to pursue anyone this far before. Usually Logan caught them right up the road from where they'd started.

As Ben pulled slowly on to the bridge, he hit his lights in anticipation of darkness once inside the wooden overhead. There was Logan, jackknifed inside, just at the other end. Ben did the same and slid from the driver's seat. The rider slowed quickly, looking as though he might hit Logan's SUV, then turned and looked at Ben. He had the demeanor of a trapped animal and Ben was afraid he might do something stupid.

Logan switched on the loudspeaker and stepped out of the SUV.

"This is Sheriff Will Logan. Step off the bike, put it in the standing position, and place your hands on your head."

Ben couldn't shake the feeling that this bike thief was desperate to get away. He worried for the kid's safety. The guy wasn't that big. Ben figured him for his early teens. As Ben made his way closer, he held his hands up and spoke softly. The kid sped past, taking his chances he'd slip by, but swerved into the truck instead. The bike came to a full stop against the truck on impact, sending the kid over the wood beams and into Grove River.

"We've got to get down there!" Ben yelled.

The two of them climbed into the SUV and took off down river to look for him.

"There," Ben said, pointing.

The rider floated aimlessly along the current, which rushed toward a small drop. Ben looked downstream at the much larger drop, praying they'd get to him well before then.

"We'll meet him there," Logan said, pointing up at the next overhead pass and quickly called for an ambulance to meet them.

Ben was too anxious for the kid's life to even notice the frigid water.

"We'll catch him as he goes by," Logan yelled above the rushing water. They waded as quickly as possible to the middle of the River. They hardly had time to brace themselves as the water propelled the rider right at Ben. As he made his way to the water's edge, something in him suspected this was not just another catch.

"He's just a kid," Ben yelled, as they pulled him to the grass.

"Correction," Logan said as he pulled the helmet off, "*she's* just a kid."

"Lord in heaven, what am I supposed to do with *this*?" Ben asked.

2

Genuine Enemy

BEN SAT OUTSIDE THE hospital room of the young girl who'd stolen his bike. Fish. That's what they were called until Consuming Fire got a hold of them. He couldn't call her a fish. It seemed somehow undignified and inappropriate. He wouldn't press charges of course, he never did, but he knew he couldn't put a little girl out on the weekend. Distracting would be the least of the problems it would cause. What on earth would he do with this little minnow? He couldn't just let her go without any thought for her restoration. He'd have to look around and find a proper program for her.

"Lord, what did you mean by sending her to me?" he whispered. "Help me find the right place for her."

"Are you going to drop all charges?" Logan asked, holding his hat in both hands.

"I suppose."

"What do you think about starting a girl's weekend?"

"Not entirely certain that's my calling Sheriff."

"I'm going to change into some dry clothes, why don't you do the same?"

"I think I'll just wait a bit and see if she wakes up."

Ben sat outside her room until he was chilled to the bone in his wet clothes. He'd begun to nod off to the news on the overhead TV when a nurse came by and tapped him gently on the arm. She tilted her head to the side, pushed her brows together, and smiled at him, so he knew what was coming. It was the same way women had smiled at him at Rosie's funeral. There was something wise in the design of women outliving men, he thought, if for no other reason than not having to receive one of their sympathetic smiles.

"I suppose visiting hours have passed?"

"Yes, but you can come back in the morning if you'd like."

"Much obliged, thank you."

* * *

Ben stayed up half the night doing research on where best to get help for his little minnow. There just didn't seem to be a program that suited her. His growling stomach reminded him that he hadn't eaten since breakfast at Annie's. In the midst of all the excitement he must have forgotten the sandwich in the cooler. If he ate that sandwich now it would sit on top of his chest until morning. No he certainly wasn't twenty anymore. He reached for a couple of soda crackers and called it a night.

"Thank you God for all the blessings of this day, frightening as it was. Thank you for all the peace and comfort you place deep into the hearts of those whom you call your own. Please help me to find a place for that little girl, and help her to heal quickly. I pray that you would become a permanent part of her heart if you're not already in there."

He yawned and said little more before nodding off.

* * *

Ben didn't know if he should show up with flowers or a stern lecture. This was unknown territory. Had Rosie been there, she'd have known just what to do. Deputy Jensen was posted outside her room when he got there and Ben looked at him sideways.

"Is Logan making this much of a fuss over that little girl?"

"Told me to stay outside the room until we can identify her—says you're welcome to press or drop charges."

"This won't take long."

He prayed with everything in him that he'd know what to do and walked into her room with nothing but trust.

"Hey there," he said softly.

She fluttered her beautiful green eyes and looked over at him.

"You gave me quite a scare young lady."

"I think you're in the wrong room," she snarled and closed her eyes again.

"I don't believe so. You stole my motorcycle yesterday and crashed it into my truck while trying to make your getaway. I would like to speak with you for a moment."

"Where am I going?" she asked, pulling on her wrists, which were handcuffed to the sides of the bed.

Ben grabbed a chair from the corner and sat at her bedside. "I'd like us to begin with a prayer."

"Are you nuts or something? Don't sit there praying by my bedside like I'm at death's door!"

"Okay, okay," he said chuckling. "Let's just talk."

"About what?"

"About you. About how you ended up in that river."

"What do *you* care?"

"What would you say if I told you that I do?"

"I'd say you were a liar or after something."

"Are those my only options?"

She looked him over as though he were nothing special.

"Realistically."

"What if I told you that I left that key in my bike, hoping to catch a thief?"

"I'd say you're even crazier than you look."

"How old are you?"

"Why? You like young girls?"

Her angry tone filled his heart with a sadness he hadn't felt in a long time. When a young man displayed this kind of disdain Ben knew how to handle it. The proper balance of love and discipline was all a young man needed to succeed. Most of the young men Ben came across were simply lacking in one or both those areas and he was good at providing either. The anger flowing from this little girl seemed misplaced and unpredictable, which made him uneasy. The situation was so perplexing Ben was almost comfortable walking away from her. Consuming Fire was only a couple of days away and he'd convinced himself that she belonged anywhere but with him.

"Why don't you just get out of here?" she spewed.

"Usually there's a contractual agreement. I'd let you off the hook and you'd buy yourself a weekend with the other fish," he thought aloud.

"I said leave!"

"Girl-fish? Can't do that I suppose," he muttered, as though she weren't even in the room.

"You one of those old men who's obsessed with little white girls?"

She watched his expression change with a number of slurs and comments she carelessly tossed his way.

"I see I have your attention now," she said smiling.

Ben shook with anger for the first time in what seemed like forever. He stood quickly, as the metal chair beneath him fell back, crashing to the floor.

"Don't you dare take aim at me with those obscenities!"

She smiled at him, relishing the idea that she'd gotten the better of him.

"Just because you weren't taught any better than to speak like an abhorrent fool, hoping to shock everyone, doesn't mean you should!"

As he tore off down the hallway he could hear her laughter behind him. Ben thought it sounded like the laughter of a demon-possessed jackal.

"Ben, what do you want to do about the charges?" Jensen called out. But he needed to clear his head.

Ben suspected this was the unmistakable thing he'd felt growing closer for the past few months. He ordered a cup of black coffee and sat down to pray. His emotions ruled until he allowed his faith to minister to him. She wasn't the enemy. As usual, he'd simply come in disguise. The real foe was the desire to take his eyes off of what was important. It was that thought which sent Ben from the hospital cafeteria right back to her room.

"I have a deal for you young lady."

"I thought we established that I'm not your lady, good sir."

"Smart aleck huh?"

"I'm quite good at it actually."

"The way I see it, you can take your chances before a judge, or you can listen to the deal I'm offering."

He pulled at his sleeve and checked his watch.

"How long would I be locked up? Because the way I see it—"

"I'm not going to wait all day," Ben said.

"Doing a little time just might beat the deal of some crazy old man."

He smirked at her as he swirled the last of the coffee around his cup and tossed it to the back of his throat. The smile faded from her lips as he threw the cup into the garbage can.

"Fine, be a smarmy little pain in the neck. I have neither the time nor the inclination to indulge you. Maybe standing before a judge will change your attitude."

"I guarantee I'll be the same smarmy, little pain in the neck in front of a judge as I am right here."

"I have no doubt," he said, closing the door behind him.

"So?" Jensen asked.

"Let Logan find out where she belongs and I'll check back on Monday."

"You got it Ben."

* * *

Cameron had grown tired of his mother riding him around the clock. In a way he'd missed the security of knowing he'd do well on a test, or the gratification that went along with being trusted to keep his word, but those days seemed long behind him. His mother seemed serious about her threat to send him away to live with his grandparents. After the year he'd had since his father died, there was no way he was going to allow even one more change. If keeping the peace meant making a phone call to some dork his aunt Raquel knew, so be it. He dialed the phone and turned down the stereo as he took a sip of cold beer.

"This is Cameron Stowe. May I please speak with Bill Jeremy? I believe he's expecting my call."

Cameron rolled his eyes and pulled a clean shirt from the closet.

"Hello Cameron, this is Bill."

"My aunt Raquel asked me to call you."

"Of course. She and I have a mutual friend; Ben Gerard."

"I don't really know all the particulars, I just want to make my mother happy."

"Okay."

"She's had a hard year," Cameron said, after an awkward silence.

"The way I understand it, it hasn't been an easy year for you either."

Cameron wasn't about to let some random, do-gooder work his way into his head. He hadn't meant to bring up anything about the past year.

"You a shrink or something?"

"No," Bill chuckled, "No, I'm not. Just someone who wants to help if I can."

Yeah right, Cameron thought.

"Well, I don't want to take up your time. If you could just pass on the message to my aunt or your friend or whoever that I called you, that would be great."

"Tell you what Cam, get a piece of paper, write down this address and meet me tomorrow."

"For what?"

"Just two guys getting together."

"I already have plans tomorrow and I hate being called Cam."

"It sounds like I've upset you. I didn't mean to."

"How could you upset me? I don't even know you."

"Good. I have a prior commitment this weekend, but what about the coming week?" Bill asked.

It sounded like this guy wasn't going to give up.

"I'm slammed this whole week Mr. Jeremy, so, I don't think a little excursion with you is going to work for me right now."

"I'll tell you what, keep my number handy and when you have some time give me a call."

"Well that sounds like a blast," Cameron said, as he gulped down the rest of his beer and tossed the can in the corner.

"Cameron?"

"Yes Bill?"

"I'm sorry about your dad. I lost my dad a few years ago and it was one of the hardest things I've ever gone through. If you find that you want to talk about it, you know how to reach me."

"Duly noted."

He threw the phone to his bed and hurled the pen against his wall. Who on earth did that guy think he was, calling him Cam and wanting to swap stories? He turned up his stereo and slammed his closet door shut.

* * *

Twenty semi-familiar faces stared at Ben from the picnic tables outside the sheriff's station. He made it a point to try to memorize something about each one when he'd first spoken to them so they wouldn't seem like strangers when the weekend came around.

"Present and accounted for?" Logan asked Ben.

"Twenty men, all present and accounted for."

Sheriff Logan nodded at him and then turned to the men.

"You would all do well to listen this weekend and heed the advice of Mr. Gerard. It may seem like he got you into this, but in reality you got yourselves into it, in most cases long before he came along. I'll turn you over to him now."

"Thank you Will," Ben said, shaking his hand.

No matter how many of these weekends Ben had done, there was something unique about each of them, even though Ben always planned the same itinerary.

"I am Ben Gerard. I know we've all met but I've found in almost any situation it's best to start at the beginning. In the past year every one of you committed a crime against me worthy of legal action. At some point after the crime was committed I came to each of you with a contract, willing to strike a deal. In return for dropping the charges, you agreed to come and spend the weekend with me and all these other men. There will also be a team of brothers I've assembled to assist in what will be known as the beginning of your restoration, should you choose to let it be that. I'm not going to get into specifics with you here and now, except to say, your presence here means you've signed a contract with me giving your word that you would resign yourself to the weekend fully, with no questions asked. The reason I'm reminding you of this is because you may find this part difficult to submit to."

"I don't submit to men!" Anthony yelled.

"True that!" someone agreed.

"Would you rather go to jail?" one of the other men taunted.

As laughter and jeers began to erupt, Ben realized he'd better take control.

"What I mean by submission may be something unfamiliar to you all, but I'm hoping and praying that by the end of the weekend you understand a little more about it. I need you to trust me for any of this to work. You agreed to accept my terms for this weekend, so you wouldn't be charged with a crime. Now I'm asking you to go a bit further with me. Listen, not as though I am one who wants to do you harm, but as though I am a friend. I know you're not ready to see me that way yet. Please don't mistake my extended hand for weakness. You will be expected to keep your word, as the contract stipulates. Incidentally, a kept word is evidence of integrity. Should you choose at any time *not* to keep your word, your agreement will be annulled and you will be escorted off of the weekend and taken back to the sheriff's station. Nothing beyond this weekend will be expected of any of you. On Sunday evening you will be driven back to this very location and free to go."

Malachi pulled up in the big blue bus, took the fishing line and hook from around his neck, and hung it over the rear-view mirror. He pulled his cap down on to his head and nodded at Ben through the glass.

"Gentlemen, you board this bus as strangers. You may hear yourselves referred to as fish that took the bait. Don't be offended by this, it's simply a part of this weekend's journey. Whatever events happen from now until Sunday are no one's business outside of the weekend. Some experiences you have out there may be profoundly life changing and some may be just plain silly. Whatever this weekend turns out to be, it belongs to you and no one else. This weekend can be the greatest or the most distressing of your life. It may be something you ponder in your heart for years to come, or nothing of the sort. Before we can get started, you must leave all contraband with the officers to my left. Anyone found holding these things, will immediately nullify their contract and be escorted back here. So that there is no confusion, I will tell you what that contraband is now. There are to be no cell-phones. Please call whomever you need to right now and say goodbye until Sunday. I want your full attention. Do not bring alcohol. Do not bring anything pornographic. Do not bring any illegal drugs, that means anything you intend to smoke, swallow, sniff, snort, drop in your eyes, breathe in, inject, look at, listen to, or *think* about, which physically altars your state of consciousness. I already have a list of prescribed medications, which will be dispensed accordingly by our team."

Ben went on against the railing moans and groans to which he'd grown accustomed over the years.

The men lined up to hand off various bags and even pillow cases full of items deemed unsuitable, to the waiting officers. He noticed one of the younger fish, Frankie, looking at him as though he was terrified. Ben had done this enough to know why.

"These officers will not go through your bags, even if they suspect there may be something illegal in them. Your bags will be placed in lockers and returned to you on Sunday evening, unharmed and untouched. For this one weekend and in this brief moment, think of them as your friends."

Frankie swallowed and wiped the sweat from his forehead. Ben caught his eye and nodded, trying his best to assure him that it would be all right. Frankie handed the bag off and glanced at Ben one more time before boarding the bus.

Once everyone was seated, Ben shook hands with both officers and climbed into the bus. He was sure to make eye contact with each man and began the weekend, the way he had each one before it.

"Therefore let us be grateful for receiving a kingdom that cannot be shaken, and thus let us offer to God acceptable worship, with reverence and awe, for our God is a consuming fire."

He looked over at Malachi who nodded and pulled the bus doors closed.

"We all right Mal?"

"We're all right Ben."

3

Consuming Fire

THE CAMP WAS AS beautifully manicured and welcoming as ever. Bill held his four-year-old daughter Iris in his arms and they both waved at the men as they rolled up between the shade trees.

"Gentlemen, welcome to Farrow Island's, Camp Trinity. That is Pastor Bill and his little Iris waving to you on the right hand side of the bus," Ben said.

The men all looked out the window, some were seemingly un-im-pressed, some waved or smiled at little Iris.

"Coming up on our left are your sleeping quarters for the weekend, also referred to as the men's dorms."

"That mean there are *ladies'* dorms somewhere nearby?" Dylan asked.

"I hope so!" Trevor called out laughing.

"That'll do," Ben said, standing to address them all. "Pastor Bill and his family live on the grounds. Their home is just up the path. There are private signs posted all around, which would be hard to miss. At no time on the weekend is anyone to go anywhere he isn't invited. I usually dispense this little chat at suppertime but since you asked where to find the ladies, I thought I'd save us all the suspense and tell you now. There are no ladies out here while Consuming Fire is taking place. Bill's wife Olivia and daughter Iris will leave this evening after supper and they won't be back until Sunday after we've gone."

Ben pointed to the church out of the front window of the bus.

"That's Living Word Church. Bill is not only the caretaker of this camp but is also the pastor of its church. They have a congregation of about four hundred, but it's ours alone until Sunday morning."

"Yippee." Trevor whispered.

"Yeah, who's going to sleep tonight, knowing that pretty little church is just up the road?" Dylan snorted.

"You don't have to raise your hand son," Ben said to Frankie. "What is it?"

"What's that thing you said? Consuming Fire?"

"Didn't you read the contract moron?" Trevor spewed.

"Please don't refer to one another with insults or anything of a provocative nature. Frankie, Consuming Fire is the name of this annual weekend," said Ben.

He faced them all again and pulled on the door handle.

"Please head toward the men's dormitory and find your room. Feel free to unpack, wash up, and make yourselves at home. Each room is equipped with two beds and every two rooms share a bathroom, so you'll share a room with one man and a bathroom with three. We will spend much of our time in the conference room, which is located in the rear of the building. Whenever we convene in this room I call it a roundtable meeting, mostly because there's a big round table in the middle of the room. Gentlemen, I'll see you soon."

* * *

Olivia zipped up Iris's bag and rolled it to the front door. She waited for Bill to wrap up his phone call with Cameron so they could have a proper goodbye.

"I'm sorry for being disrespectful toward my mother and I promise it won't happen again," Cameron said, looking at his mother, who stood in his bedroom doorway with her arms folded.

"Did someone force you to make this phone call?" Bill said, slipping into his shoes.

"Yes."

"Do you have any interest in our spending time together?"

"Not really."

"So, if we don't get together at this point, you'll be in trouble with your mother?"

"Yeah."

"Tomorrow I'll swing by your place and pick you up. If you don't want to kill yourself after an hour or so with me, I'll treat you to lunch and drop you back off at home to keep you from the wrath of mom."

"Do you need my address?"

Cameron couldn't believe he'd asked.

"Yes," Bill said motioning for Olivia to hand him a pen. "You'd better sound more disappointed if you want her to buy this."

This guy wasn't getting in, but he wasn't bad.

* * *

Ben waited patiently for the men to get settled into what would be their quarters for the weekend. By the time they made it over to the common building for dinner the place smelled like heaven.

"Gentlemen please take a seat and bow your heads," he said to them.

Dylan looked around the room at everyone as Ben thanked God for their meal. Most had their eyes closed while some looked down at their feet.

Lucius found it difficult to eat. He was too distracted by the bustle of the team members. Some dished out extra food while others took drink orders for lemonade, iced tea, water, or coffee. They joked with each other as though they were thrilled to be there.

Frankie hardly looked up from his plate.

"Do you know something I don't?" Lucius asked.

"What do you mean?" Frankie said, when he finally stopped eating long enough to look at him.

"Is this our last meal for the weekend?"

"No, it's not," said Malachi.

He'd come up between them to drop off another chicken breast on Frankie's plate. When he looked at him, Malachi smiled at Lucius as though they'd always known one another.

"I don't think they mean to starve us," Lucius whispered.

"Not taking any chances," Frankie said, and kept eating.

Ben walked over to the platform and tapped the microphone.

"Gentlemen, I hope you've enjoyed your supper. I'd like to introduce you to Rick McCready, your head chef for the weekend."

Rick stepped out of the kitchen and wiped the sweat from his forehead with his apron.

"I know these men would like to thank you for the delicious dinner," Ben said, clapping.

The applause certainly wasn't thunderous. It never was at this point. Rick nodded and grabbed a glass of iced tea from the cart as Oscar rolled by.

"Are any of you familiar with the Bible verse I quoted back at the sheriff's station before we left?" Ben asked.

Dylan looked around to see if anyone would speak up. Surely he couldn't be the only man in the room whose grandmother had taught Bible lessons.

"It was a verse in the book of Hebrews," said Ben. "It will likely be referred to many times on the weekend. When you go back to your rooms, you'll each find a Bible on your bed. I would like you to go to that verse and underline it. You'll first look up the book of Hebrews, the way you would any section of any book. You'll turn to chapter twelve and verses twenty-eight and twenty-nine. If any of you have questions I'll take them now."

"Why are we here if the weekend hasn't started yet?" Neil asked. "It's only Thursday."

"The weekend *has* started. Tonight is a very important part of the time we will spend together."

"Are you going to tell us why you've brought us all the way out to this island?" Brian asked.

"I can tell you the itinerary if you'd like, but it won't make sense to you."

The men murmured amongst themselves, until Ben grabbed hold of room again.

"I know you may be feeling a little regret at this point for having signed the contract. Just keep reminding yourselves that all I'm asking of you is three days and three nights. If you'd gone before a judge, who knows what you may have been sentenced to. Some of you may not be first time offenders, though it's none of my business, and you are not obligated to share that information with anyone here."

"But you're the one who set out that bike like it was bait and trapped us. If not for you, we wouldn't owe anybody anything!" Robert yelled.

Lucius stood slowly and pushed his chair back until he'd commanded the attention of the entire dining room with his six-foot-five, three hundred-fifty pound stature.

"Mr. Ben may have put that bike out on the road, but you and I didn't have to take it," he said.

His voice was soft and gentle. Ben found it an amazing contrast to his size.

The dining room grew quiet and Lucius sat back down.

"Here are your instructions for the rest of the evening," Ben said. "Look up that Bible verse and underline it. Give some thought to what it means to be consumed. Remember that you and I played a small role in getting you here. I set out the bait, you took it, but in reality, God is the maestro of this weekend's orchestra. Sometime between tonight and Sunday you might hear something that causes you to change direction. What you're doing here is really no mystery. Have a restful sleep. I'll see you for coffee at the round table in the morning. Goodnight."

* * *

"Fishing again?" Malachi asked, sitting Indian style beside Ben in the grass. He patted Roofus on the head and the old dog yawned.

Ben could see Malachi's white teeth stabbing through the darkness. He turned toward him and set a pile of line and hooks at his feet. They'd done this so many times that tying those hooks to fishing line in the darkness was hardly a challenge.

"You must need a new one by now," Ben murmured.

"Nope," Malachi said, biting down on some line. "Still good as new."

"Decent group of men," Ben said nodding.

Malachi let out a small whispery laugh as he tied off the next hook.

"I say something funny Mal?"

"You always say the same things."

"In general conversation or on these weekends?"

Malachi thought about it for a minute as he picked out another line of string and bit it off at just the right length.

"Both."

"Smart-aleck. What do you think about Lucius?"

Malachi sat quietly tying off knots for a long span. One of the things Ben admired about the kid was his thoughtfulness.

"I think guys like Lucius are the reason we do this. I also think you got a fish out of water in the shadows at four o'clock," he snickered.

"Roofus, why do I keep you around if you can't even tell me when someone's out of bed?" Ben asked.

"Fish are so predictable," Malachi whispered to himself.

Ben headed over to the tree, which moved and then stayed very still.

"Malachi," Ben yelled, so that whomever was hiding in the tree could hear him.

"Yep," he called back, still working the hooks.

"I gave the men instructions to finish the evening in silent meditation right?"

"Yes sir."

"Did I mention to them that there was to be no leaving the camp?"

"Uh . . . I don't remember if you did. Why don't you tell it to me again and I'll see if it rings a bell in my brain."

"I believe everyone was told to stay in the dormitory unless specific permission was given to leave."

"Yeah, that sounds familiar," he called back.

"Did I mention the extensive dormitory library?"

"Yeah you did Ben."

The tree hadn't moved, and Ben was determined, as always, not to lose one on Thursday night.

"Mal?"

"Yeah Ben?"

"Did I also mention the two officers located at the camp entrance, who stand guard all weekend?"

The tree shook as someone took off running, and Ben watched the door to the dormitory close as they went back inside.

"Now you know that last part's just a big old lie," Malachi said chuckling, as Ben took a seat beside him again.

"Just cut me some line," said Ben.

4

Of Fish And Men

"WELCOME TO THE FIRST roundtable meeting gentlemen," Ben said, taking his seat. Each day has a theme and a question of its own. You may have heard yourselves referred to as fish. With that in mind, I would like you to give some thought to today's question. Why be a fish?"

"What on earth will we do at these meetings?" Neil asked.

"We'll do what one does at any meeting, we'll discuss the things that matter most. You may be amazed by how quickly the time has gone by."

Lucius picked up the pen in front of him and flipped through the blank pages of the notebook beside it.

"The notebooks and pens are yours to keep," Ben assured them. "You may write down whatever you think is worth remembering. I'm at an age where I sometimes get an idea and five minutes later I can't remember where in my brain I've put it."

"When I agreed to come for the weekend. I figured I would be in some kind of lockup," said Frankie.

"What if I told you this was it?" Ben said.

"All you want for dropping the charges is to talk to us?" Frankie asked.

"Is that so hard to believe?"

"Well yeah," said Frankie. "It's hard to believe that you're not gonna punish us."

"Speak for yourself," said Dylan. "This is punishment enough."

"No one here is going to berate, punish, or condemn you," Ben explained. "No one here is even going to judge you for what you've done. Most of the men serving you on the team also traded charges for a weekend out here at one time or another. What I want, more than anything, is for all of you to know that the grace I am extending to you, is nothing in comparison to the grace of God."

Frankie sat back in his chair, sighed, and looked over at Lucius who was staring down at his own notebook.

"I just figured this whole thing out," Dylan said, smirking. "We are all supposed to become good little Bible toting boys who turn their lives around and come back to serve the next group of hapless victims they drive out here to rescue from themselves."

"Suppose you're right," Ben said, narrowing his gaze on him. "What are you going to do with that?"

"Are you asking if I'll be a different person? Change my life?"

Ben nodded.

Dylan let out a snort, as he considered seriously for a moment what he'd just said in jest.

"Why would I? Why should I? For you? For them? For God?" he said, pointing toward the ceiling.

"Surely you realize that the person most affected by your decisions will be *you* Dylan."

He glared at Ben.

"While Dylan ponders that thought, let's open this meeting with a prayer. Would anyone else like to pray?"

It was not Ben's way to use intimidation to get anyone to pray aloud. Like Bill had said for years, he suspected God would rather they came willingly. He waited for a moment and when no one responded, he prayed.

"Father, I want to thank you for your love today. I know you love us every day, but today I find myself particularly thankful. Please bless our time together. I pray that our discussions would be pleasing to you. In the name of Jesus, amen."

"Why do you always say, in the name of Jesus?" Shane asked.

"Because he was God's son," Frankie answered.

"*Was* God's son?" Ben asked. "Anyone care to expand?"

"He was God's son, but he died. They killed him right?" Fred asked.

"Crucified him," said Frankie.

"In reality, it was not a they, but a we, who killed Jesus. His death was a very important one. Does anyone know why?" Ben asked.

Oscar and Gene opened the doors, stirring the silence like a pebble in a lake. They pushed a cart of snacks and drinks.

"You pay them to be this happy?" Dylan asked, snapping open a ginger ale.

"I don't pay them, they're all volunteers," Ben said. "Let's stay on task here."

Lucius pointed to a bag of potato chips and an orange soda.

"Can anyone tell me why the death of Jesus is unlike any other death?" Ben said.

Dylan cleared his throat and took a sip of his ginger ale.

"Jesus's death was important to Christianity because it's widely believed that he's not only the son of God, but also God himself. Christians believe in a triune God, of which, Jesus is son, whose role was to be born to a virgin as a sacrificial lamb, and after living a sinless life, gave that life on the cross as atonement for the sin of all mankind. It is their belief that no one gets to heaven without trusting that he died for their sins."

He looked at Ben, raised his brows, and smiled before taking another sip of his soda.

"*Their* sins?" Ben asked.

"What's that?" said Dylan.

"You said *their* sins, as though it doesn't also apply to you."

Dylan shrugged.

"He was right about all of that. There is one important thing that he didn't mention though," Ben explained. "It was personal. I want you to imagine you're the only person in the world who's ever had a bad thought or done a bad thing. Jesus still would have let them nail him to that cross just for you."

Lucius stared at Ben, who returned his gaze and then kept going.

"Jesus, after having been crucified and dead for three days, arose and came back to walk the earth a little longer, before disappearing in a whirlwind back to heaven."

"You really believe that happened?" Trevor asked.

"No way could something like that happen. It's just a legend that got blown out of proportion," said Pete.

"No, I think it really did happen," said Frankie. "I'm pretty sure that's why we have Easter Sunday."

"He literally got sucked up into the sky?" This is what you believe Frankie?" Pete said.

"I don't know. I guess."

"Let me ask you all a question," said Ben. "How many eye witnesses does it take to get a conviction?"

"One!" They called out in unison.

"Right," Ben said. "It takes only one. There were over five hundred people who saw Jesus die and then come back to life again three days later."

"That's how they knew he was God," Frankie said, almost in a whisper.

"That's how we know it too," Ben said. "This isn't some tale in a book from long ago. This is prophecy, foretold well in advance of a coming king, who would save humanity. This is prophecy being fulfilled, at his birth, with his miracles, and at his death, and resurrection. Jesus is very much alive. He's seated at the right hand of his father in heaven, and he wants more for you than you can ever want for yourselves."

Lucius picked up his pen and wrote the word, alive, across the entire first page of his notebook.

* * *

Cameron Stowe looked like any other kid when Bill picked him up for lunch. Cameron's mother looked at them from the porch and Bill nodded at her as Cameron opened the door to Bill's convertible and they pulled off.

"Does she always look that angry?" Bill asked.

"Yep."

"Because of you?"

"I guess."

"What are you gonna do about that Cameron?"

"Gee Bill, I don't know."

"You want to know what I'd do? Bill asked.

"Is there any way to get you *not* to tell me?"

"This should be a delightful afternoon," Bill muttered.

* * *

With each passing hour, most of the men became more familiar with one another. Some shared stories about how they grew up while some talked about plans they had for the future. In keeping with the premise of the weekend, Ben brought each discussion back to God's desire for them. Lucius observed without saying a word. Dylan said nothing after his sermon on the role of Jesus.

* * *

"I can order whatever I want?" Cameron asked.

"As long as it's on the menu." Bill told him.

"Duh."

"Do you always talk to people this way?"

"Look, I don't know what your deal is, maybe you have some super-man complex, but you don't get to climb inside my head just because my aunt is concerned that I might ruin my life."

"Do you think you're going to ruin your life?"

"Don't know, don't care."

"I think you *do* care. If you don't then you should. Losing your father had to have been the most profound loss of your life so far, but it happened. What do you think he'd say if he were here and saw your grades slipping, or heard the way you talk to your mother?"

"I'll have the lobster," Cameron said.

Bill handed the waitress both of their menus.

"We'll take two burgers and two sodas."

"I thought you said I could get whatever I wanted."

"They only serve lobster at supper time. Are you going to answer me son?"

"Don't call me son."

"Are you going to answer me Cameron?"

"Why don't you back off? What do you want me to say? My father would have hated seeing my grades slip. He knew how smart I am. He knew what I'm capable of. He believed I could be anything, but what's the point now?"

"You can still be anything Cameron. Your heavenly father still loves you, still hopes for you, and still knows how smart you are."

"Oh, you're one of *those*. See, that just goes to show how alone I really am. My father didn't believe in all that life after death garbage and neither do I."

"How did your father die?"

"Car accident. I guess God was out on a coffee break huh?"

"Are you saying you would have believed there was a God if nothing bad ever happened in your life?"

"No. I wouldn't have believed, because there is no God."

"What if there is?" Bill asked, taking a sip of his soda.

"I'd say, if there *is* a God, and he wants me to believe in him, taking the greatest man I've ever known was not the best way to begin a dialogue with me."

"Who do you suppose it benefits for you to believe in God?"

"I don't know. Probably guys like you. Supermen who get some kind of an incentive by recruiting people."

"Well, I guess I won't be getting my toaster today," Bill muttered.

* * *

"Gentlemen, I have enjoyed getting to know you this morning," Ben said. "I hope you've given some thought to today's question."

The common building awaited them, coated in the scent of dinner. The team hustled about, getting the food on the tables.

"Fish on deck!" Rick yelled from the kitchen, as they entered.

"Good evening," Malachi smiled, greeting them at the door. "Which one of you wants to be my Holy Mackerel?"

They looked around at one another.

"You look like *you* can hold your own. You'll do," Malachi said, pointing at Lucius. "Answer one question."

"Okay," said Lucius, sounding unsure.

"Why do fish end up in our coolers, in our freezers, and on our plates?" Malachi asked.

"Because they're delicious." Trevor said.

"Easy! Cause they get caught!" Frankie yelled.

Malachi looked at Lucius and raised his brow.

"Are either of those the answers you think I'm looking for?"

Lucius glanced over at Ben as perspiration began forming on the back of his thick neck. He shook his head at Malachi but didn't say anything.

"Because they're stupid?" Brian said.

Lucius looked Malachi in the eye.

"I suppose it's because they take the bait."

He spoke so softly that Ben had to quiet everyone down.

"Could be I've found my Holy Mackerel," Malachi said. "Keep going."

"A fish can't help taking that bait!" Frankie yelled. "He's just hungry!"

Lucius kept his stare on Malachi.

"So what's that poor fish gonna do not to end up on your plate?" Malachi asked Lucius.

"If he's *not* on your plate then he didn't take the bait," Lucius said.

"Why's that?"

"He's no longer a fish," Lucius whispered.

"How does he know he's no longer a fish?"

"He doesn't act like a fish anymore."

"You think that's how it works Lucius? If we act like good boys, does that make us good boys?"

"Not really."

"Then how does he know he's no longer a fish?"

"Maybe he doesn't feel like a fish anymore."

"Can a fish stop being a fish because he doesn't *feel* like a fish?"

His eyes filled, but he never broke Malachi's stare.

"Maybe for the first time in his life, someone told him to walk," said Lucius.

"Why would a fish learn to walk?"

"Because now he's a man."

"You mean, he was dead and now he's alive?"

Lucius nodded.

"Holy Mackerel gets his choice at dinner!" Malachi yelled.

"What are we having?"

"Fish."

Lucius sat back observing the new world he'd been thrown into where pride was ones ruin and humility ones greatest strength. He concluded that anything he had was only valuable if he was willing to give it away. Come Sunday, he wasn't sure he'd *want* to leave.

* * *

That night, when Ben dismissed them, he asked the men to write down all the wrong words they'd either thought, or heard someone else use to describe them.

Lucius sat at the small desk in his dormitory room and stared out the window.

"Long day huh?" Frankie asked.

"Yeah."

"You know what you're gonna write down?"

"Thinking about that now," said Lucius.

OF FISH AND MEN

"My mom's first husband called me spaz. Should I write that down?" Frankie asked.

"I guess."

"I never really understood anything about God. I guess I never bothered to find out if all that stuff was for me," Frankie admitted.

"What do you think now?" Lucius asked.

"I think . . . why keep doing all these things I've *been* doing? Because it's just easier to do what you know."

"What about doing what's *right*?" Lucius asked.

"Who are you my priest all of a sudden? I'm writing down *spaz* and I'm going to bed. Night Lucius."

Lucius picked up his pencil and opened the notebook on the desk in front of him. Before long he'd assembled a list of horrid slurs and statements, most of which had been heard in childhood. Though he'd never thought about it until that moment, the insult which most stood out to him was the word, *nothing*. As he looked at it, the word seemed to stare back at him, as though it wanted to run from the page.

Lucius climbed into bed and sobbed in the darkness with a heart full of love.

5

From Fish to Fishermen

BEN STOOD AT HIS seat, ready again to address the men.

"So far we have talked about who God is, what you wanted to be when you were boys, how men become fish, and a man is certainly *not* supposed to become a fish."

Some of the men chuckled at that statement.

"Last night I asked you all to write down words that have been used to wrongly describe you. I am now going to offer you an opportunity to say goodbye to those words."

"How is throwing away a piece of paper going to change anything?" Dylan asked.

Ben eyed him as Oscar and Gene pushed the doors open. This time they wheeled in a wooden cross. Gene held a hammer in his hands and Oscar, a handful of heavy-duty nails. After the wheeled the cross to the front of the room, they stood on either side.

"When we are hurt as young boys," Ben began, "it can cripple us. If you were in a wheelchair, people would certainly know you had an ailment. Being emotionally crippled is far worse. You can't put your finger on it, but you know something is broken. Some of you may have been walking with an emotional limp for so long that by now you've gotten used to it. The physical act of ridding yourselves of those wrong ideas just might rid you of that limp."

"Okay," Dylan said, and laughed. "What does that mean here on earth?"

"I'm asking you to nail the things, which have kept you from succeeding, to this cross. You needn't be concerned with these untruths any longer. Today you are free to say goodbye to being fish and become fishermen,"

Ben said, pointing to Malachi, who stood just off to the left of the cross with the hooks they'd spent Thursday night tying onto fishing line.

Lucius stood and walked toward the men with a torn out page from his notebook.

"No longer nothing," he said, taking the hammer and a nail without hesitation.

He stood there for a moment staring at the nail-driven list he'd pinned to the cross, then walked over to Malachi and bent down far enough for the fishing line to be placed around his neck. He looked down at the hook that hung from the line and smiled at Malachi.

Frankie looked around at all the other men and then ripped his page out and jogged up to the cross.

"I'm not a spaz," he said.

He nodded at Oscar and Gene and then took the hammer and nail to stake his page. He looked back at Lucius and smiled as Malachi placed a fishing hook around his neck.

One by one, the men lined up to shed their scales and accept their new roles as fishermen.

Dylan finally made his way over with his page folded in half.

"Do I have to say what I wrote out loud like the others did?" he asked Ben.

"Of course not Dylan," Ben said. "How much you share is entirely up to you."

Dylan sighed as he took the hammer in his hands and then nailed the folded piece of paper to the cross. Malachi eyed him as he placed the hook over his head.

Once all the men had nailed their deepest struggles to the cross, Ben stood in front of it.

"From now on, you might try letting *God* define who you are," he said.

* * *

Cameron fastened his seatbelt and looked over at Bill.

"For two people who have nothing whatsoever in common, we sure see a lot of one another."

Bill laughed and nodded.

"I suppose that's true."

"Where are we off to today?"

"You mean your mother didn't tell you?"

"No," Cameron answered, furrowing his brow.

"I have to drop off some supplies to a friend who runs a homeless shelter."

"Let me guess, my mom thought I'd do well to see some people less fortunate than I am, thereby planting a seed in my ungrateful heart."

"Yep. You caught us Cam. There we went trying to make you feel grateful."

"I *am* grateful."

"You are? For what?"

"I'm not an idiot. I realize I have much more than a lot of people. I'm not feeling sorry for myself."

"No one said you were."

"You didn't have to. It's in your eyes. This kid has it made. This kid is having a pity party just because his father died. This kid needs to get over it."

"Think you may be projecting just a bit?" Bill said, grinning.

"Yeah, maybe."

"For the record, I think you're just going through a rough time and though I appreciate the compliment, I don't think my eyes say quite that much."

"Gee Bill, they're such a nice deep blue," Cameron said, with a chuckle.

"You're funny."

* * *

"Please leave your notebooks and pencils and follow me," Ben said.

"Where are we going?" Frankie asked.

"This is my favorite part of the weekend journey. We are going to take the rest of the afternoon off and go fishing."

"I thought we had to spend the weekend studying the Bible. I didn't know we were gonna get to have fun."

The men all followed Ben out of the building and through the trees. They walked along the cement pathway, which led down to the dock, where a boat waited for them.

"Whose boat?" Dylan asked.

"For the moment, ours," Ben said smiling. "I'm glad you like it."

"If you need someone to drive it, I can do that," Dylan offered.

* * *

Malachi sat back with his feet up, though he kept an eye on Dylan, who steered the boat with ease and excitement. This was the first time all weekend Dylan seemed happy, and Malachi thought giving up driving the boat was a small price to pay for that.

"Do you really think having faith means not having any fun son?" Ben asked Frankie.

"I don't know. I never had fun in church, that's for sure."

Ben patted him on the back the way a father would. Frankie raised his eyebrows at him.

* * *

Cameron didn't make a secret of the fact that he wanted no part of being at the homeless shelter. He felt badly for people who were less fortunate, but he wasn't going to let it shake him.

"Can you give me a hand?" Bill asked, as he parked the car and got out.

Cameron followed him to the trunk and Bill handed him a large box, then he grabbed the other and shut the trunk.

"This way," Bill said, opening the front door.

Cameron followed Bill down the hall, which opened to a larger recreational type room. Some kids were playing table tennis. Cameron noticed many of the paddles were broken. He stood there with the box still in his arms, while Bill shook hands with some man Cameron guessed to be the director of the God-forsaken place.

"I see you've brought a helper," the man said looking at him.

"This is Cameron," Bill said. "Cameron, this is Mr. Torres."

Cameron put the box on a nearby table and shook his hand.

"You wouldn't be interested in volunteering a couple of days a week would you? Community service looks great on a college application."

"One after school special is enough for this kid, Cameron sighed."

"I don't understand," Mr. Torres said, smiling.

"Cameron has a mental disability, which precludes him from working with people."

Cameron wiped his hands on his pants and glared at Bill.

"Bill, can we go over some numbers for next month?" Mr. Torres asked him.

"Of course. Hang out Cameron, we'll be right back."

"Fantastic," Cameron said under his breath.

He could see them talking through the window in the office and wondered how long this would take. He thought perhaps he should wait in the car and turned to leave, but when he turned around, there was a boy standing behind him. The kid couldn't have been more than six or seven.

"Look out," Cameron said, nearly tripping over him.

"Can I have mine now?" he asked.

"What?" Cameron said.

The boy pointed at the box and Cameron shrugged.

"You're barking up the wrong tree kid," he said, heading for the door. He stopped at the drinking fountain and when he turned around to leave, he noticed a bunch of the kids had gathered around the boxes, which Bill put on the floor. He was curious, but not enough to go back in.

When Bill finally made it out to the car, Cameron was almost asleep.

"Get your feet off my dash," Bill said.

"Finally! Man, do you know how long I've been sitting out here?"

"No one forced you to come outside."

"What was with that crack about my being mental?"

"You were being rude to Mr. Torres."

"Great, so some guy I don't even know thinks I'm a mental case. What was in those boxes anyway?"

"Shoes."

Cameron played back the picture of the kid in his mind's eye. He had been standing there in his socks. Cameron hadn't realized it in his haste to get out of there.

"Who was that kid who was talking to me?"

"Which kid?"

"Blonde hair, brown eyes, freckles."

"Jack. Great kid."

"No shoes? Seriously?"

"You find his situation too cliché?"

"I didn't mean it like that."

"Haven't you ever known anyone who lacked bare necessities?"

"Let's not turn this into a bonding moment Bill. And don't tell anyone I'm mental . . . ever."

"You mean you'd like to be treated with decency and respect?"

"Duh."

"I will if you will."

When Bill pulled up to the curb in front of Cameron's house, he wondered if he'd ever see the kid again. It had been a long silent ride home.

Cameron got out and leaned over the door, letting his hands dangle through the open window.

"So, *why* didn't Jack have shoes?"

"His father died and they had no insurance. They lost their house, their car, everything."

"I'm assuming he'd had shoes before that."

"Yes Cameron he had shoes. He outgrew them and his mother couldn't afford to buy him another pair."

"What about family? Grand parents?"

Bill shrugged and shook his head.

Cameron nodded. He tried to fool Bill into thinking he couldn't care less, but suspected it would be rough getting the memory of Jack's face out of his head.

* * *

Before anyone could ask whether they would be expected to catch their own lunch, Ben gave Malachi a knowing nod and Malachi told Dylan he would take over driving the boat. They had been out in fairly deep waters all morning, getting to know one another and far less guarded than they were at the Roundtable Meetings. Some of the men even joked about how much better it was to be fishermen than fish.

"Gentlemen, shall we dine?" Ben asked, as they pulled toward the dock on a small island. Just beyond the seawall in the grass was a blue canopy, and beneath it a long table was set for lunch. The white linen looked as crisp and welcoming as a fine restaurant. Each water glass was already filled, and each salad bowl had been chilled for them.

"This is living," said Trevor.

"I can get on board with this," said Dylan.

"Salad? But I'm starving," Frankie moaned.

Oscar laughed and pulled the chair out for him.

"The rest of the meal will come later buddy, just sit down and relax."

Lucius couldn't help but look up at the canopy above his head. It was made of some kind of transparent material. He could see straight through to the sky and yet they were protected from the sun. He had never seen anything like it. The water was beautiful too, shining back at them after a long morning on the lulling waves.

Ben said a prayer for each one around the table and for the gorgeous day out on the water. When he finished, he noticed more bowed heads than there had been previously. He was happy about that, and thanked God silently for grateful hearts.

"What else are we having?" Frankie yelled out, taking the last bite of his salad.

"Don't be rude," Lucius whispered.

"What were you hoping for?" Ben asked Frankie.

"I don't know. A cheeseburger maybe?"

"I hope you're not disappointed with the menu then. Gentlemen, surf and turf."

A low roar of excitement began to build, as Oscar and Gene went to retrieve the rest of the meal. Ben folded his hands together, pleased, but then he noticed Frankie didn't look any happier than when he thought he would only get a salad.

"You're not satisfied with the lunch I chose for us today Frankie?"

"I don't know. I never heard of that surf thing."

"It's probably steak and lobster, brainless," Dylan yelled out from across the table. "I just hope we have a nice bottle of bubbly to go along with it."

Oscar placed a steaming tray of stuffed lobster tail and filet mignon in front of Dylan. The lobster tail had been rolled in seasoned breadcrumbs, baked, and was sliced and placed back inside the shell with melted butter. The steak had been pre-cut for them, into thick, juicy, chunks.

"What kind of meat is this?" Frankie said, almost yelling. "You don't even have to chew it!"

"Frankie man, calm down," Lucius said.

"Let me know what you think of the lobster as well," Ben said.

"Yeah well, if he doesn't want it, I'll eat his," Dylan smirked, holding out his glass toward Gene, who re-filled it with iced tea.

* * *

The men gathered in the chapel, showered, clean-shaven, and glowing from the sun. Ben looked at each of their faces with hope.

"Gentlemen, it's been a long day, but one I hope you'll remember for years to come. Bill is going to take us on a journey, but first, we are going outside to do something very important," said Ben, and they followed him out the door.

Malachi stood over a fire pit with a barbeque lighter in his hand. Inside the pit were all the papers that had been nailed to the cross that morning. The men gathered in a circle around the pit and looked to Ben.

"Today we got rid of many things which have held us back and tonight we will burn up those misgivings as an offering to God," Ben announced. He gave Malachi a nod to set fire to the pages. The men stared in silence as the fire quickly ignited, taking with it all the things they had given of themselves. Malachi couldn't help but notice the one folded page had flipped open in the blaze. It was blank. Dylan looked at the open page and then at Malachi, who was staring back at him.

* * *

Bill took his place at the podium once again. What Ben most admired about him was his tendency to exclude himself from God's righteousness. Bill never intimated that he had some special place in God's kingdom, kept only for clergymen. He spoke the gospel in simple truths mingled with a self-deprecating humor that most seemed to appreciate. There was never any pleading, guilt, or manipulative ploys to get them to hand their lives over to God. Bill insisted that having faith was the smartest, most logical, as well as the simplest thing to do. Ben wondered if Bill would bring up the fact that he'd made the first weekend, no more than a thief himself. Sometimes he mentioned it in his talks, sometimes not. He wrapped up with a prayer, naming each of the men aloud. He didn't always do that either and Ben liked it when he did.

"Okay," said Ben. "Tonight you get to process all that you've heard. More importantly than my forgiving you and wanting to be your friend, you've learned that God, the very creator and sustainer of all that exists, wants to be your friend. There is nothing you can do to make him love you any more or any less. There is nothing you can do to make him love you any more or any less than anyone else. He loves you, not because you are worthy, not because you promise to be a good person, but because he is a loving God, capable of tremendous compassion and mercy. A divine love like God's cannot be reasoned with, it cannot be taken advantage of, and mere man cannot comprehend it. Pastor Bill is available for counsel if you need him. See you all in the morning friends."

The word, *friends*, resounded in Lucius's ears as he walked to the kneeler at the foot of the cross and fell to his knees.

* * *

Cameron threw the rest of the beer to the back of his throat. His mother had been asleep for hours. Taking her car had become no big deal to him. He wasn't supposed to drive after eleven at night and he was never to drive if he'd been drinking. He stepped outside quietly closing the door behind him.

* * *

Ben sat in his room contemplating the close of another Consuming Fire weekend. In the morning some men would confess their faith, some wouldn't. Ben knew that reality well by now. He dared not ask God to see every seed come to fruition. He simply did what he knew to do and left the rest. On the heels of that thought was the reality of a little girl who was handcuffed to a hospital bed a few miles away.

* * *

That couldn't be the right time. Bill squinted to get a better look at the dim, blue, neon glow in the corner of his bedroom. It was after midnight and his phone was buzzing like mad on the night table.

"Hello?" He mumbled, clearing his throat.

"Bill? I need help."

"Cameron?"

"Can you come to me?" Cameron asked, with a shaking voice.

"I'm on my way," Bill said, rubbing the sleep from his face. "Text me the address."

* * *

"You do that?" Bill asked, motioning toward the tire-marred begonias and mailbox, which now lay parallel to the ground.

Cameron's mother's car looked as though it had a bit of damage on the front end, but Bill supposed it would be fine there for the night. Had

Cameron not looked inebriated he would have taken a look at it then and likely gotten it started.

"I suppose."

"You either did or you didn't," Bill said, raising his brows.

"Yeah."

"Been drinking tonight?"

Cameron thought about lying, but what was the point?

"Yep."

Bill headed toward the front door of the house.

"Where are you going?!" Cameron asked, hurrying behind him.

"We can't just leave without letting these people know what's happened."

"Wait . . . no . . . Bill!"

Bill knocked on the door and Cameron heard him apologize and then promise to return in the morning to repair the damage. Cameron couldn't figure out why he'd taken the blame for something he hadn't done.

"Thanks for the lift. You can drop me a couple doors down so I don't wake my mother."

Bill pulled the car in front of Cameron's house and turned off the engine.

"Just tell me what I have to do so you won't report me to my mother. Should I buy Jack a second pair of shoes?"

"I'll have to think on that Cam. In the mean time, you may be too intoxicated to realize that you have no choice but to tell your mother what's happened. In the morning, she will likely notice that her car is not in the garage."

Cameron moaned and lifted himself from the passenger seat.

"Don't call me Cam."

6

Fishers of Men

"GENTLEMEN," BEN SAID, GATHERING the men to attention once again. "Pastor Bill is willing to baptize any of you who wish to be baptized."

"I want to be baptized," Frankie called out.

"Me too," said Shane, and when Ben looked at him, Trevor nodded. Ben knew the majority of the men would simply go back to their lives, but he hoped they would at least reflect on the gospel and think seriously about the things Bill had told them over the weekend.

"Very well then," said Ben. "Let's head down to the river. I would like everyone to join us, including those of you who do not wish to be baptized."

"The Bible claims that there is one Lord, one faith, and one baptism," said Bill. "At Passover, the lamb's blood was placed over the doorways of the homes of the Israelites as instructed by God. Those children were saved as they slept. The gift of faith is just that, a gift."

"If faith isn't about us then why baptize at all?" Shane asked.

"We are simply following God's instructions. The same way the Israelites did at Passover. The lamb's blood still saves today the way it did then."

"So it's a symbol then?" Trevor asked.

"It's much more divine than that," Bill said. "Obviously we cannot know the mind of God. Whatever is done during baptism and communion is a mystery, but a means of grace nonetheless."

Lucius stepped forward and looked down at Ben. One might have missed the warmth in his eyes in light of his stature. Ben didn't. He kneeled down in the water and Bill held him with one hand while tipping him backward with the other.

"Lucius Mobley, I baptize you into the kingdom of God, in the name of the father, the son and the holy spirit."

Lucius arose from the water with a broad smile and grabbed Bill, pulling him close. The two embraced, while knee deep in the water.

When the last man was baptized, there erupted a round of applause, save for the men who opted to forgo the ceremony. Dylan emerged from that group and began to trudge slowly through the sand. When he got to the water's edge he looked up at Ben, squinting against the morning sun.

"I want to be baptized as well," he said, meeting Ben's gaze.

Malachi sat in the sand nearby with his knees drawn up to his chest. Dylan looked over at him and smiled.

* * *

Ben stood at the front of the dining room.

"This morning I'd like to offer you all a chance to share your weekend experience with everyone if you choose to do so."

He pulled the microphone to the center of the room and turned it on, then took a seat beside Malachi.

"We all right Mal?" he asked smiling.

"I don't know Ben."

"What's wrong?"

"Something doesn't sit right," he said, motioning toward Dylan with his eyes.

Dylan saw them looking at him and gave a nod.

"Is there something going on between you two?" Ben asked.

"We were locked up in Juvey together when we were kids."

"You never told me that," Ben said, studying Malachi's face.

"I didn't want to sway you one way or the other about him."

"Don't underestimate God Mal. This weekend may be the first time Dylan has ever heard about grace. Besides, what motivation would he have for playing pretend on the last day of the weekend?"

"Don't know the answer to that one Ben."

"Hold that thought," Ben said, as he pointed to the podium.

Lucius stood in the center of the room with his notebook in his hands. He placed it on the podium, looked down at the open page, and finally raised his eyes.

"Today's the first day since I been here that I aint confused."

Some laughter broke out and Ben found himself chuckling as well.

"When I climbed the steps of that big blue bus I figured we was headed to a work camp. But then we came to this beautiful place. When I saw the conference room I thought it was gonna be like in school, when you get detention. Instead Ben told me God loved me. People brought me snacks and drinks like I was a rich man. When I saw my notebook I thought I was gonna to have to write down an apology. I figured I was dead in the water because I've never been no good at writing. If I had to write something I knew Ben would cancel his agreement with me on the spot. When I showed up for dinner on Friday night they asked me why a fish ends up in a net. I was scared to answer, figuring if I said the wrong thing, I was going back to the sheriff's station. All I had was the truth, so I said the truth and that seemed to be good enough. Saturday I nailed something to that cross that I been carrying around for a long time. I still figured I would get something wrong and they'd kick me out of here, but at least I put those words where they belong. I was wrong just about every time I tried to imagine why I was here. Instead of punishing me, he cared for me, instead of starving me, he fed me, instead of calling me a crook, he called me his friend."

Some of the men began to clap, but Lucius didn't move from the podium.

"I'm not talking about you," he said, looking at Ben. "I'm talking about God. Six months ago I found out I had a little girl, but I never did get to meet her." Silence fell over the room as the weight of what he was saying took hold. "Her mama met somebody else and let him believe he was Kayla's daddy. Kayla . . . that's my little girl's name . . . she fell in a pool and drowned."

Tears streamed his face but he didn't bother to wipe them away. Rick came out of the kitchen and stood in the midst of the dining hall to listen. Having lost his daughter when she was only eighteen months old, he found that he could feel Lucius's pain from where he stood.

"The only time I ever got to see her, she was already lying in that little white casket. Her mama told me I could come to the funeral and say my goodbyes. She showed me pictures of Kayla. She took after my Granny a lot in the eyes. After the funeral, I started feeling pain like I never knew before. That pain covered me . . . like a blanket. It was there when I went to bed at night. It was there when I woke up in the morning. I asked God for help for the first time in my life. Then I saw that bike with the keys in it—I guess I got the idea in my head that I could drive it off a bridge and stop that pain."

Ben tilted his head and furrowed his brow.

"See, I thought that bike was an answer to my prayer. And it was . . . just not the way I thought."

After Lucius finished speaking, the room erupted in applause. Malachi hurried to the podium and embraced him.

Bill Stood at the front of the dining room and held up a small loaf of bread.

"We will now have communion together," he said. "Sharing in Christ's body and blood is no small thing. We are not made worthy to receive God by anything we have done. In fact, we would be foolish to conclude that we are ever holy enough to receive God. Our conclusion should be that God is holy enough to dispense himself to us, though we are unworthy to receive him.

"After supper had ended, Jesus took the bread, blessed it, and broke it," Bill said, tearing the loaf in two. "Then he said, this is my body, which is broken for you. As often as you eat it . . . remember me." Bill handed the pieces to Ben. "After that he took the cup and said, this is the cup of my blood, shed for you, and for all, for the remission of sin." Bill held the cup high for a moment and then handed it to Malachi.

Frankie walked up first and looked at Ben. Ben nodded at him and he tore off a piece of the bread.

"Christ's body broken for you," Ben said, smiling at the boy.

Frankie stepped to the right and Malachi held out the goblet of grape juice.

"The blood of Christ, shed for you Frankie," Malachi said.

Frankie dipped it carefully and stuck the piece in his mouth.

When Lucius stepped forward he looked down into Ben's eyes and smiled.

"The body of Christ, broken for you," Ben whispered.

Lucius pinched the bread loaf, tearing off a piece but never broke Ben's stare. With his free hand he reached for Ben's wrist and squeezed it as they looked into one another. Ben had been present for yet another seed coming to fruition before his very eyes. Lucius stepped toward Mal and smiled.

"The blood of Christ, shed for you my brother," Malachi said to Lucius, choking back his tears.

Lucius dipped his bread into the goblet of wine and nodded, pushing it into his mouth.

One by one, the men filed down the line and shared in communion, while the men who had opted not to be baptized waited for breakfast.

CONSUMING FIRE

Over the years Ben had noticed a dividing line at Sunday's breakfast, drawn clearly between the men who had confessed faith and the ones who would leave feeling relieved that the weekend was over. The men who had been baptized and taken communion together always seemed to gravitate toward one another. Ben reasoned that they now shared something that drew them together, turning them from strangers to brothers. He and Malachi had learned to eat breakfast with the group of men who wanted to leave, to keep a sense of unity until the close of the weekend.

* * *

When he arrived at Cameron's house, Bill could hear Mrs. Stowe yelling at her son through the front door.

"You lied to my neighbors and covered for Cameron when he wrecked their mailbox? What kind of a pastor are you?" she squawked at Bill.

"Good morning," Bill said, opening the door and stepping inside. "I thought it was the right thing to do under the circumstances."

"Lying about a minor drinking illegally, taking my car without permission, and crashing it was the right thing to do? I'd hate to ask what you consider wrong-doing."

"If you have some coffee, I would love a cup," said Bill. "Maybe we can talk about your son and how best to handle him."

She unfolded her arms and shook her head.

"Decent men who care about the welfare of my son seem to be in short supply these days," she said, heading to the kitchen. "Not that I'm certain you're one of them."

"I think Cameron is having a harder time dealing with the death of his father than you realize," Bill said, reaching for the cup she placed in front of him.

"That excuse is getting really old, really fast," she smirked. "I am sending him to live with my parents for a while."

"Is that the only solution?" Bill asked.

"The only one that springs to mind."

"Let me offer another, and then I'll leave you to think about it while Cameron and I go to repair the damage he did with your car last night."

"I'm all ears."

"Let me have a shot at the kid."

"Excuse me?" Mrs. Stowe said, shaking her head.

46

"Give Cameron to me until school starts up again in the fall."

"To do what?" she asked, re-folding her arms.

"I'm sorry. I'm talking about taking your son, and I don't even know your first name," Bill said.

"Angela. You'd like to take him to do *what* exactly?" she demanded.

"I'm not entirely certain. Let's call it a work program. I think that Cameron has lost a great deal—not just a father, but a constant encouragement, and a champion."

"Yes," she whispered, closing her eyes.

"I suspect that if he really believed someone else was in his corner, it might re-instill in him a desire to behave like it. Before you answer, just think about it," Bill said.

* * *

"Gentlemen, this will be our final Roundtable Meeting of the weekend," Ben said, taking a seat. "Many of you have heard terms over the past few days, which may be unfamiliar. Now is the time to discuss these things. I've invited our team to sit in on this last meeting so we can discuss the weekend together."

"What happens now?" said Frankie.

"What do you mean?" Ben asked.

"I mean, I can't go back to my old life, but to be honest with you, I have no other way to make money and my girlfriend's pregnant. What do I do for my family?"

"I assume you were making money illegally?" Ben asked.

"Let's just say, people count on me to get things from one place to another," Frankie explained.

"If you don't mind working like a dog, I can use someone to help me," Rick said. "It's manual labor, but most days I'll be working right along side you, and I'll pay you pretty well if you earn my trust and work hard."

"Like doing what?" Frankie asked.

"I'll give you my number," Rick promised. "If you're serious about heading in a new direction, call me."

"If I was to get into ministry, could I count on some kind of financial support from you or your people?" Dylan asked.

The hair on Malachi's neck stood on end.

"Let's not get ahead of ourselves," Ben said. "Don't you think maybe you ought to learn some more before you go trying to start a ministry of your own?"

"My grandmother taught me everything I ever needed to know about the Bible. All it took was this weekend to shake it loose from my heart."

"Be that as it may," Ben started.

"Tell us when it happened," Malachi interjected.

"Pardon?" Dylan asked with a smile.

"This divine revelation, that gave you a sudden burning desire to go into the faith business. Tell us exactly how that transpired," Malachi pursued.

All eyes were suddenly fixed on Dylan. The room was silent as everyone awaited his response.

Dylan chuckled but looked straight through the kid.

"Well that's sort of a personal thing, isn't it Malachi?" he shot back.

"No, see, it isn't," Malachi said, returning his stare. "When God grabs someone and shakes him, that someone wants to share the story. That someone can't help telling it."

Dylan narrowed his eyes at him but said nothing.

"Oh, my mistake," Malachi whispered. "I suppose I just let the cat out of the bag."

"Mal?" Ben asked. "What do you mean son?"

"I just told him how to fool more people with his fake ministry. Though I suppose he'd have figured it out sooner or later on his own."

* * *

Bill pulled up to the house and stopped the car.

"Should we get out and do something?" Cameron finally asked.

"We?" Bill said, reclining his seat. He settled into the corner against the door and closed his eyes.

"You're going to sleep?" Cameron asked.

"Yep," Bill murmured. Someone woke me up in the middle of the night."

"So what am I supposed to do?" Cameron asked.

"Fix the mailbox."

"With what?"

"Tools are in the trunk."

"What makes you think I know *how*?" Cameron asked, raising his voice.

"Push the post upright, fill in the empty spaces with dirt, pack it in . . . viola," Bill said, with a yawn.

Cameron got out and slammed the car door shut behind him. Bill reached down and pulled the lever for the trunk then readjusted in his seat. He knew he wouldn't sleep, but the kid needed the lesson. He wondered what he was going to do if Angela decided he could stay out on the island with Bill for the summer. He figured all Cameron needed was a little hard work to put him back on track.

After he finished with the mailbox Cameron put the shovel back in the trunk and slammed the trunk closed.

"I'm done," he said, getting back into the car.

Bill sat up and wiped his eyes.

"Now what?" the kid asked.

"Now we fix your mom's car," Bill sighed.

"That's all you, I know nothing about cars."

"Well, today you're going to learn a little something."

* * *

Cameron stood against the wall listening just outside the kitchen. He couldn't believe his mother was considering sending him to stay with this guy, but if he went to stay with his grandparents, he would be far from his friends and he'd have to enroll in a new school. He'd lost enough already.

"If it doesn't work out, you can still send him to live with his grandparents," Bill reasoned.

He watched her weighing both options. He knew any decent mother would be at least a little hesitant to send her son off with some guy she hardly knew. While he didn't need another project right now, in his gut, Bill felt like he could help.

"Beneath all that anger, he seems like a good kid. If you send him off you could push him even further away," Bill pointed out.

Cameron was surprised by Bill's statement. A virtual stranger seemed to understand him better than anyone.

"What's your wife going to say about this?" Angela said, almost smiling.

"Liv is the most understanding woman on the planet. She'll probably go too easy on the kid. But don't worry, I'll be hard enough on him for the both of us," Bill said, with a wink.

"Suppose I just say no to both living arrangements?" Cameron said, sauntering in. "I'm almost a grown man, you can't really make me do *any-thing* I don't want to do."

Angela looked as though she didn't have any idea what she would do at that point.

"That's entirely up to you Cameron," Bill said, "but then your mother will press charges against you for stealing her car and you can take it up with a judge like a grown man."

"My mother would never do that," he said, smiling.

Angela gave Bill a pathetic look. He pushed his brows together and nodded at her.

"Yes I would," she said. "It's Bill, Grandpa, or a judge . . . choose."

* * *

"I would like to thank each and every one of you for giving me the opportunity to get to know you better," Ben said. "It's my every hope that the grace of God be with you all, whether you already realize what God has done for you or if it happens upon you some time down the road. We will have a follow-up dinner in two weeks, mainly to catch up and share the experience of going back out into the world. At that time you can let Malachi know if you're interested in being a part of a Consuming Fire team in the future. You are under no obligation to come to the dinner. Many former fish come to share a laugh and some fellowship or even for support. May God bless you and keep you."

7

Blythe

CAMERON HAD HEARD ABOUT Camp Trinity. He'd even been out to Farrow Island when he was a kid, but he hardly expected it to be so lovely.

"Kind of neat place isn't it?" Bill said, pulling on to the grounds.

"I had no idea there was this kind of money in the God business," Cameron said.

Bill chuckled and waved at Mal and Ben as they passed in the big blue bus.

"Who are they,?" Cameron asked, eyeing the bus full of men.

"They are the hope of a better future."

"Wow, pretty deep stuff Bill."

He pulled in front of his house, turned off the car, and looked Cameron in the eyes.

"I want you understand some things before we go in."

"Well I suppose I'd better put on my thinking cap then," Cameron said, as he shifted sideways in his seat to meet Bill's stare.

"I have invited you into my home, with my wife and daughter. If at any time you behave disrespectfully toward either of them, I will take that very seriously."

Cameron smirked and narrowed his eyes.

"I would think hard before you say whatever it is you're about to say. I'm a pretty relaxed person, but don't confuse kindness for weakness, especially where Liv and Iris are concerned."

"Should I curtsy or would you rather I bow when I meet them?" Cameron said, chuckling.

"Either will do. Perhaps curtsying would be more fitting though. At least until you've learned to behave like a man. You can carry your own bags," Bill said, getting out of the car.

* * *

When they brought Kaitlyn Blythe out to Ben, she looked hardly any different than the first time he'd looked into her cold, green eyes.

"Long weekend?" Ben asked.

"You talking to me old man?"

"Yes."

"Don't.

The officer holding the clipboard looked more than a little annoyed with her.

"Been in and out of the system most of her life, looks like. Foster homes mostly, then group home for the past two years, till she ran off for a joyride on your bike."

Ben looked her up and down. She looked too small and scrawny to have caused so much trouble.

"Anything to say for yourself, young lady?" Ben asked, raising his brows.

She stared straight ahead in silence.

"Charges on the bike will be your call, but she'll have to deal with the state for reckless endangerment, and driving without a license."

Ben looked at the officer and nodded.

"Do you have any family?" Ben asked.

Kaitlyn looked at him as though the very word were foreign to her.

"Uncle Sam, Mother Nature, Father Time. I've got family all over the place."

The officer shook his head.

"They're sending someone from the Department of Children and Families to come get her."

The officer put her in a holding room and Ben looked at her through the glass. He firmly believed there were no accidents. He was certain God had brought her into his life. Ben simply had no idea why.

"What will happen to her now?" Ben asked.

"She'll go back to the group home, probably run away a few more times. She'll age out of the system soon anyway."

"Sounds as though that doesn't bother you much," Ben said, still looking at her.

"Don't mean to sound callous," he said, "I've just learned that it's a part of the job."

Ben couldn't help but feel as though she wasn't beyond reaching.

"Drugs?" Ben asked.

"Nope. Not yet anyway."

He was relieved to hear that. Addiction was a whole different animal.

"It's just a matter of time with kids like her. Sooner or later she'll screw up badly enough to end up dead or behind bars," said the officer.

Ben knew the officer was right, statistically, about kids like Kaitlyn ending up dead or in jail. While he couldn't help everyone and he certainly couldn't put a little girl out on a Consuming Fire weekend, he couldn't shake the feeling that there was something more he could do. He prayed for guidance and then picked up the phone.

* * *

Cameron followed Bill to his office upstairs. It was less than half the size of his room at home. There was a desk and a couch, a floor lamp, and a small closet.

"It's not much, but it's the only vacant room in the house," said Bill. "The couch folds out and it's actually pretty comfortable."

"Great," Cameron said sighing. "I suppose I'm expected to fold it up immediately upon waking and report downstairs at 0600 for calisthenics?"

"Technically, there are no house rules. I guess we'll cross that bridge when we come to it . . . and I hope we don't," Bill said, with a half smile.

"Can I ask you a question?"

"Shoot," Bill said.

"What are we hoping to accomplish with this little maneuver?"

"A change of scenery, while your mother gets her head together."

"This feels like it's more about me than her."

"I'm not going to lie to you Cameron, it *is* about you. I know you're grieving. I know you're pissed off, but have you once stopped to consider how difficult this time is for your mother?" Bill asked.

"Duh."

"Then why make it harder than it has to be?"

Cameron tossed his bag into the corner and pulled out his phone.

"May I please have some privacy?" he spewed.

"Liv and Iris are coming home soon. Dinner's in an hour or so," Bill said, closing the door.

Cameron plopped on the sofa and looked around Bill's office. Why on earth would this guy invite a virtual stranger into his home? Maybe if they'd met under different circumstances he'd have liked Bill, Cameron thought, perusing the pictures on the desk. He wondered what his father would have thought of Bill—probably that he's too religious. Cameron looked at the cross hanging on the wall. *You're not getting inside my head either*, he thought.

* * *

The scent of dinner began to rise to the second floor and Cameron heard a car door slam. He pushed the blinds apart with his fingers to get a look. Iris jumped from her car seat and ran to Bill. He picked her up and she threw her arms around his neck. Olivia pulled a bag from the back seat and Bill stopped her, pulling her into them both instead. The three of them embraced as though they hadn't been together in ages.

"Well, isn't this a picture-perfect moment," Cameron whispered.

Iris ran inside and Bill pulled the bag from the back seat while talking to Olivia. She glanced up at the windows and Cameron jumped back.

"Cameron, come down and meet my girls," Bill called, once they made it inside.

He sauntered down the stairs with one hand stuffed in his pocket.

"Hi," Olivia said, smiling at him.

"This is Olivia," Bill said, "and this is Iris."

Iris hid behind her father's leg and peeked out at Cameron.

Olivia was much prettier than Cameron had expected and their daughter looked like a miniature version of her.

Bill narrowed his brow, reminding Cameron to be polite.

"I'm Cameron," he said, extending his hand.

"Iris?" Liv asked, "Can you say hello to Cameron? He's going to stay with us for a while."

She stayed behind her father's leg.

"Hi," she said, quickly hiding her face again.

"Okay," Bill said, lifting her up to place her in her booster seat. "Your chair awaits."

Bill pointed at one of the chairs and Cameron sat down, while he and Olivia put the rest of dinner on the table.

"Iris, would you like to pray tonight?"

She shook her head and eyed Cameron.

"No? Who should pray tonight?" Her mother asked, straightening Iris's dress.

She pointed her little finger at her father.

"Are you going to pretend you're shy because Cameron's here?" Olivia asked.

"All right," Bill said, "Daddy will say the prayer tonight."

Cameron watched them all close their eyes as Bill thanked God for the safe arrival of his girls, another Consuming Fire weekend, whatever that meant, and then finally the food.

* * *

It seemed Kaitlyn wasn't exactly a troubled kid; at least not to begin with. Her parents had died when she was five. She had a brother who was just a baby at the time. With no close living relatives on either side, they became wards of the state and were separated within months. Her brother would be ten by now. Ben wondered if he'd been placed as an infant. Perhaps he didn't even know he had a sister. It seemed an awful lot to lose at such a young age. It was no wonder her heart seemed so cold. He took a gamble that if she remembered she had a brother, it might be a good place to begin.

* * *

"Okay Cameron, follow me," Bill said, heading out the door.

Cameron followed behind as they walked through the trees and down the lane to the men's dormitory where Ben's fish had spent the weekend.

"What is this place?" Cameron asked.

"This is a facility we keep for retreats and getaways."

"So what are we doing here?"

"We're here to clean up a little," Bill said.

"Isn't there a cleaning service that can handle this?" Cameron asked.

"Actually, there's a team of men who served here all weekend and they do a fairly good job of making sure the place is clean before they leave, but I come in after just to tidy up anything left undone," Bill said opening a door.

"Like what?"

"Like scrubbing out the toilets," Bill said, handing Cameron a toilet brush.

"Fantastic," Cameron whined, "a genius IQ saved for scrubbing toilets."

"A genius IQ who *earned* this task by stealing his mother's car," Bill smirked.

* * *

In the early afternoon, Ben arrived at the children's home where Kaitlyn lived. He hoped to get inside her head, though she had given no indication of that happening.

Molly Bivens was one of the daytime caretakers. Logan had arranged for Ben to meet with her, since there were strict rules about who could see the children in the home.

"The kids usually get excited about a visit, but I wouldn't expect too much excitement out of *that* one," Molly said.

"Yes Ma'am," said Ben, taking a seat.

When Kaitlyn came around the corner, Ben stood with his cap in his hands. Her hair was disheveled, her shirt, which looked more like it belonged to a boy, was torn at the corner, and her jeans were shredded at the bottom.

"Hello again," he said, and smiled.

"Holy coyote! Look everyone," she bellowed. "It's my long lost uncle. He's come to tell me I'm an heiress who's inherited the family fortune!"

"That'll do!" Molly scorned.

"What's the matter Molly? Don't you see the family resemblance?"

Molly shook her head and went back to her paper work.

"Maybe he's my sugar daddy," Kaitlyn laughed.

"You enjoy shocking people don't you?" Ben asked.

"What do you want old man?"

"For starters I'd like you to call me Ben."

"I won't be calling you *anything*," she said, and started back the same way she'd come in.

"Wait," Ben pleaded. "I came to show you something."

"Right here in front of everyone?" she said winking at him.

"Stop that. Come and sit down."

"What is it old man? I got a full day going over here."

Ben held out a file and handed it to her.

"What's this supposed to be?"

"Open it up and find out," he said, hoping she would at least be curious about her brother.

She looked down at the file and back up at Ben, before tossing it at him, until the papers spilled out all over the floor.

"Don't come back here!" she yelled, walking away.

"Can't say I didn't warn you," Molly said, helping him pick up the papers.

"I just wanted her to see it for herself," he mumbled.

"Surely you know that child can't read?"

"No . . . I didn't. Why on earth can she not read? She's got to be at least fifteen-years-old."

"These kids have no interest in their studies. Most are just doing time here until they age out."

"Then what?" Ben asked.

"Then they get a hundred dollars and their walking papers."

"With no job? No experience?"

"Job? Most of them can't even read a bus schedule, never mind get a license or anything else."

"What happens to them?" Ben asked.

"Usually they blow through their money in one night on a room or food and end up on the streets the next day. The smart ones go to a shelter and try to get back into the system as adults."

"You mean with financial assistance?"

"Yes. I'm sorry Mr. Gerard, I have a desk full of paper-work."

"Thank you for your time," Ben said.

"Look," Molly said stopping him at the door. "I hope I don't appear to be cruel. This place used to break my heart wide open. I even took in a few of the kids who aged out. It always ended up the same; they'd rob me and run off anyway. It didn't take me long to realize you just can't help everyone. When I graduated I was so sure that my degree in social work was going to help me change the world. In a small way I like to think that still happens. I show up here every day, try to keep the kids safe, every now and then I hear one of them say please or thank you. I've learned not to have expectations beyond that. I'm just doing what I can, you know?"

"Yes Ma'am," Ben said, looking at the ground. "I do."

* * *

"Lunch-time!" Olivia called from the camp dining room.

"I tarried your soda," Iris said, smiling at her father.

"You did?" he asked, taking two cans of root beer from her little hands.

"See you at home," Olivia said, kissing Bill goodbye.

Cameron unwrapped his sandwich and took a bite.

"Oh, sorry, I suppose you wanted to *thank the Lord* for your salami," Cameron snickered.

"I did give thanks for my salami," Bill said, taking a bite of his sandwich. "Yours too."

"Seriously Bill, let's say for a moment that there really is a God up there somewhere who's running the whole universe. Why would he care one iota about your little thank you? I mean certainly he'd have better things to do."

"Okay—let's say there *is* a God to whom I pray, who runs the universe. It seems to me then that the universe and everything in it belongs to him. Therefore this sandwich is really his and he's letting me eat it. For that, I thank him."

"According to you then, he made all of mankind? This God?"

"Yes," Bill answered.

"Then he created you with a *need* for sustenance?"

"Obviously."

"Then what of all the people who have no food? They have need of sustenance also, do they not Bill?"

"Of course they do."

"Can we assume then that God just likes you more?" Cameron winked.

"I wish there were no hungry people, no homeless, shoe-less children," Bill said, holding his sandwich in front of him.

"See, this is where Christianity—religion of any kind, stops for me. Because not a one of you can make sense of why life sucks Bill. You all want to subscribe to something bigger—some sky-dad out there who really cares for us all. Maybe it makes you feel less alone, but in the end, the question of why life sucks stumps every one of you."

"No it doesn't Cameron. I know *exactly* why life sucks."

"Oh, by all means Bill, do tell."

"Let me answer you this way. Why are you here?"

"The logical answer, at least for me, would be evolution."

"No," Bill said. "Not, how do you think you got to this *planet*. Why are you here scrubbing *toilets*?"

"Because you're a sadist?" Cameron smirked.

"Seriously?"

"Fine," the kid whined. "Because I jacked my mother's car and went out drinking."

"Would you say then, life might be a bit sunnier today for you, had you listened to your mother's instructions to begin with?"

"What's your point?" Cameron asked.

"My point is that any Christian could tell you that we are the reason that life sucks Cameron. The question of why bad things happen is easy to answer. The presence of evil, selfishness, or human depravity doesn't nullify God."

"Are we talking Adam and Eve here?" Cameron chuckled, taking a sip of his soda.

"We are talking human nature here," Bill said.

"If you're going to use some book to argue out of that I don't even believe in, then this debate is over before it even begins."

"That's a good point," Bill said, finishing off his sandwich. "So let's start with the Bible."

"Oh no. What do you mean?"

"Have you ever read it?"

"No," Cameron laughed, "but I don't have to read a romance novel either to know that it's not for me."

"Did you know that the Bible is historically accurate? Did you know that there are scientific facts in the Bible which modern man failed to stumble upon until years after it was written?"

"Suddenly I'm longing for toilets that need scrubbing," Cameron said, wadding his waxed paper into a ball.

"Okay, back to work," Bill laughed.

* * *

Frankie couldn't have asked for a better boss. Rick picked him up in the morning, worked hard with him until sunset, and paid him in daily, before dropping him back off at home.

"Same time tomorrow?" Rick said, as Frankie gathered up his things and got out of the truck.

"Yeah, sure."

"Listen," Rick said, "There's a big job I can take, but I'm going to need you to show up for work every morning."

"Haven't I shown you that I'm reliable yet?" Frankie asked.

"Yeah, that's why I'm taking the big job. I can't do it without help, and the last guy who worked for me always seemed to call in just when I needed him most."

"Well that won't happen with me Chief. If I say I'll be there, I'll be there."

"Good. I'll pay you double for the days on that job," Rick said, handing Frankie that day's pay.

"Wow, anything special you want me to wear?" he joked. "For that kind of money I might even sing to you."

"No thanks," Rick said laughing, "I've heard you sing. See you bright and early."

"You got it. Night Chief," Frankie said, slamming the door.

* * *

"What time will the Reynolds be here?" Bill asked Olivia.

"I told them that dinner would be at six o'clock, but that they could come anytime after five."

"I'm guessing they'll be here five minutes before six, and be gone before seven," Bill said, kissing her cheek.

"She really wants him to start coming to church with her," Olivia said, stirring a pot on the stove. "So many married women come alone every Sunday. I don't know what I would do if I couldn't share my faith with you."

"Yeah," Bill agreed. "And it's been at least two years since you've had to coax me out of bed on a Sunday morning," he said, winking at Cameron.

"You're having people from church over for dinner?" Cameron asked.

"Yes," Bill answered.

"I suppose that happens a lot?"

"Liv and I try to socialize with the church folk here and there. Why?"

"Well, I heard what you said about the husband and you probably don't need me getting in the way of your sales-pitch. I can eat up in my room."

"Don't be silly Cameron, if Mr. Reynolds doesn't buy my sales-pitch, I'm going to throw your house-keeping services in as an incentive."

"Would you stop teasing him?" Olivia said. "Cameron, we would really like you to join us for dinner. Now you," she said to Bill, "please go find your daughter and get her cleaned up. Cameron, would you please slice the vegetables for salad?"

There was something about Olivia that made Cameron want to be polite. Her heart shone in her eyes. He could see why Bill adored her and Iris. As he obliged her and reached for the cutting board, he found himself wondering if he would one day come home to a woman as kind and as beautiful.

* * *

Frankie strode down the sidewalk feeling as though he owned the world. He looked down at the ring he'd just bought for Maria and smiled. If he worked hard, Rick would help him get his own accounts and equipment. In a year or two he could have his own landscaping company. He found himself truly grateful for the Consuming Fire weekend and all that it had brought into his life. He began to pray a silent prayer of thanks when a familiar voice broke into his thoughts.

"Seems you've found new employment," Chris said, closing the car door.

"Oh Chris—man you scared me," Frankie said. "Have you just been parked there waiting for me?"

"Hector isn't gonna be too happy if you don't do that Miami run."

"No, listen, I got a new job with this guy, he's gonna train me to have my own business . . . and Maria, I'm gonna marry her man."

"Hector only cares about his Miami run. He already bought your plane ticket."

"I can't go to Miami. I have to go to work. If I end up in jail I'll lose everything."

"If you don't do this for Hector, you'll lose a whole lot more than that," Chris said, showing him a blade.

"Are you threatening me right now?" Frankie asked, as the smile faded from his face.

"Not if you tell me that you're going to Miami. I don't want to do this, but Hector sent me."

"We were friends man. What are you doing?"

Another man got out of the car and held his knife out where Frankie could see it.

"Fine!" Frankie yelled, putting the ring in his pocket. "I'm not afraid of either of you. I'll take you both!"

As they closed in on him, Frankie felt his pulse racing out of control. As he prepared to start swinging he noticed the color disappear from the faces of his would-be assailants. They slowly backed away and then jumped in the car and took off.

"Yeah, that's right, you get out of here! And tell Hector I'm not afraid of him either!"

When Frankie turned to leave, he saw all six-foot-five, three hundred -fifty pounds of Lucius standing behind him.

"Whoa man you scared me," he said, bumping into his friend.

"Seems like you're not the only one," Lucius said, watching the car speed around the corner.

"What are you doing here?" Frankie asked him.

"Not sure," said Lucius. "I just went out for a walk, ended up here."

"How'd you know where to find me man?"

"I didn't. I wasn't even looking for you."

"You might have saved my life right now."

Lucius shook his head.

"Not me," he said, looking up at the sky.

"I didn't even know we lived in same neighborhood," Frankie said.

"We don't. I've been walking for about two hours."

"Well, you're coming home with *me*. You have to meet Maria. Look what I bought her," he said, pulling the ring out of his pocket. "Come have dinner with us, she's a great cook."

"She'd have to be, to be *your* girl," Lucius said, smiling.

* * *

Ben waited patiently for Kaitlyn to join him in the front room of the group home.

"She may not come out at all," Molly said," shaking her head.

Kaitlyn finally appeared in the front room and when Ben stood, she put out her hand to stop him from saying anything.

"The only reason I came out here was to tell you to stop bothering me old man. If you come back here again I'll file a complaint with the state that you've been harassing me. They don't take too kindly to old men paying unwanted visits to young girls, if you know what I mean."

She started back down the hall and Ben knew this was his last chance to reach her.

"You have a brother," he called out.

She stopped and turned around. Ben watched the contempt disappear from her face and assumed that she indeed remembered she'd had a brother.

"You found Matty?" she said, with tears welling up in her green eyes.

"No. Not yet. I didn't even know his name. Matty? Matthew is it?"

She nodded and wiped her eyes, approaching him.

"Maybe I can help you find him," Ben offered.

"If you haven't found him, how did you know about him?"

"I have a friend in the records department. I saw the file. I know about the car accident that killed your parents and that your brother was an infant when you two were separated."

"But it didn't mention his name?" she asked.

"No. Seems there was a fire and most of the records were destroyed. All I could dig up was this hard copy," he said, pulling a paper from the same file she had thrown at him days earlier.

She took the paper from him and wiped her eyes again.

"What good is this stupid piece of paper if you don't know where he is?!" She yelled.

"Calm down. I'll find him."

"How?" she demanded. "No one else has been able to tell me anything about him!"

"I said I'd find him."

"I took your bike, and now you're going to do something for me that no one else has been able to do?" she asked.

"This has nothing to do with that," he said. "How'd that turn out anyway?"

"Probably have to do some time in Juvey," she said, flipping back her hair. "No big deal."

"I have friends in the system. What if I make some calls and try to help?"

"And why would you do that?"

"I'd do that in exchange for something."

"I knew you weren't right in the head the minute I met you," she said.

"You have to stop believing that everyone thinks like you do young lady."

"I told you not to call me that."

"Kaitlyn."

"Truth be told, I don't really care for the way *that* rolls off your tongue either."

"In exchange for helping you, you let me teach you to read," Ben said.

"What on earth makes you think I even care about that?" Kaitlyn asked.

"I believe you're smart enough to know how dumb it would be to try to get out of here without a plan for your life."

"Now you're going to help me plan my life?"

"I'd think you might want to be a little better equipped. When you meet your brother, don't you want to be able to read?" he asked.

"Don't you dangle Matty in front of me. I doubt you'll find him anyway. As far as getting me off the hook with the state, I'll do my time. I'm not afraid to go to Juvey."

He nodded, put the paper back in the file, and turned to leave.

"You really think you can find my brother?" she called out to him.

He turned from the doors and looked into her.

"Yes."

"What's your angle old man?"

"Guess you'll just have to wait and see . . . Blythe."

8

Undercurrent

CAMERON COULD HEAR BILL and Olivia doing their morning devotions together from upstairs. Their faith in a God they couldn't see puzzled him. Bill wasn't foolish and he wasn't phony. In fact, neither he nor Olivia fit the pathetic stereotype Cameron assumed encapsulated all of Christendom. He lay there wondering what torture the day held for him when he heard Olivia call him down to breakfast.

"More toilet scrubbing today?" Cameron asked.

"Homeless shelter," Bill said, with a mouth full of cereal.

He eyed the kid, waiting for his usual smart-aleck reply, but none surfaced. Cameron poured a glass of juice while a picture of Jack flashed in his mind's eye.

"I want to go work with daddy today," Iris announced.

"You do?" said Olivia. "You'll have to work very hard like daddy does."

Iris giggled in her chair, making her little blonde curls bounce up and down.

"Tamron? Do you work with Daddy now?"

Cameron smiled over at her and nodded.

"I want to go with Tamron and Daddy."

"Awesome," Cameron said to her. "I need all the help I can get."

* * *

Mr. Torres saw Bill and Cameron come in and met them at the front doors of the shelter.

"Hi Iris," said Mr. Torres.

She smiled sheepishly at him from her father's arms, with her legs clinging to his waist.

"How's everything John?" Bill asked, shaking his hand.

"I don't know how we'll make it through the month with numbers like these," he said. "We're nowhere near our bare-minimum target."

"I want to play with the toys," Iris said, wiggling her legs.

Bill looked at her for a moment and glanced around the shelter.

"That's okay," Cameron said, "I've got her."

She took Cameron's hand and Bill followed John to his office.

Iris looked up at Cameron and pointed to the corner, where a little boy played quietly with a plastic schoolhouse. Cameron nodded at her and let go of her hand but followed close behind.

"Hi," Cameron said to the boy. "This is Iris. She'd like to play too, if that's all right with you."

The boy kept playing as though they weren't there. Iris looked at Cameron and he motioned with his head that it was okay for her to play too. He looked around for Jack, but didn't see him.

"His name's Emanuel," the boy's mother called from a nearby bed.

Cameron looked over at her and nodded.

"He's not being rude, he's deaf," she said. "We're learning sign language."

Cameron looked down at Emanuel, where he played in silence, as Iris chattered on about the schoolhouse.

I've got to stop coming to this place, he thought.

* * *

While Cameron buckled Iris into her car seat, Bill took out his cell to make a call.

"Rob, it's me, what have we got discretionary wise?" Bill said, as he drove them away from the shelter.

"Okay, wait about twenty minutes and then take all of that and transfer it over to John . . . thanks."

He hung up and dialed another number.

"Liv, what have we got in that other savings account? Can you ballpark it? That's all, really? Okay," he sighed. "Do me a favor and transfer it to the church discretionary account sometime in the next fifteen minutes. Thanks honey."

Cameron looked out the window and tried to figure out why a man would empty his own savings account to make ends meet at a shelter that could hardly keep its doors open. Of course, for all *he* knew, Bill might have a total of ten dollars in his savings account.

* * *

Ben wrote out a check to a friend who was a local PI, fairly certain that she would be able to track down Kaitlyn's younger brother. He gave her what little information he had stumbled upon in the file and she told him she would get back to him as soon as she found anything.

"Thank you Greta," he said leaving the office.

"I'll do my best," she smiled.

* * *

By the time Bill was done making his rounds Iris was asleep in her car seat. After emptying his own savings account, Cameron had seen him stop in to at least three people to make sure they were okay. It seemed as though everyone in his congregation needed him in one way or another. Whether someone's garbage disposal needed fixing, or they simply had family visiting and wanted Bill to drop by to say hello, it seemed a lot of people were counting on him. When at last they got home, Olivia took Iris to her room. She turned to Bill then with a smile and wrapped her arms around him. As Cameron climbed the stairs to his little office space, he couldn't help but notice that Bill and Olivia seemed to begin and end each day taking comfort in one another and in a God he didn't know.

* * *

Lucius looked out the window of the diner and took a sip of his water, as Bill and Cameron slid across from him and took a seat in the booth.

"Thanks for meeting me," he said to Bill.

"No problem," Bill said, introducing Cameron.

Cameron nodded and picked up his menu.

"Everything okay?" Bill asked.

"I'm worried about Frankie," said Lucius.

"Thought he was working with Rick McCready."

"He is—doing great too—his old boss isn't too happy about it from what I can see."

"What's given you that impression?" Bill asked.

"The other night a couple of guys came after him. They were gonna rough him up pretty bad."

"Oh?"

"Bill, if I wasn't there, he might have been killed."

"Then I'm glad you *were*."

Cameron looked over at Lucius. He found that he was mesmerized by the irony of his soft voice and gentle demeanor. He was undoubtedly the biggest man Cameron had ever met.

"You know he asked his girl to marry him?" Lucius said.

"No, I didn't. She's pregnant right?"

"Yeah. The kid's about to start his whole life . . . no one should mess with that."

"I agree," Bill said. "If need be, he and his girlfriend can come and stay out on the island until this thing with his former boss blows over."

"You know Frankie," Lucius said, "he's not afraid of nothing—even when that nothing is something."

* * *

"Didn't know your church had bouncers," Cameron said, as they got in the car.

"Lucius is not from my church."

"Not that it's any of my business, but should you be getting mixed up in these kinds of situations?" Cameron asked. "Offering refuge to ex-cons seems a little dodgy."

"First of all, I doubt Frankie would accept the invitation—he's not really the type to submit to a rescue. Anyway, I'm just giving the kid half a chance to start his life," Bill insisted.

"I just don't think you should take the chance that Olivia or Iris could come face to face with someone dangerous."

Bill smiled over at him.

"Wow Cam, a concern for others. Nice change of pace isn't it?"

Cameron shook his head and looked out the window.

* * *

Kaitlyn raised her eyebrows in surprise when Ben came back a third time.

"You find my brother?" she asked.

"I'm working on it," Ben said, taking a seat.

"Then what are you doing here?"

"Thought we'd try some reading exercises."

"Get real old man," she said, walking back to her room.

The next day, Ben walked into the group home holding a box of donuts and waited. This time Kaitlyn never came out at all. When Molly told her Ben was there to see her, she simply shook her head and kept drawing. Molly came out and relayed the same message, shaking her head as well. Ben sighed and set the box of donuts on her desk. The next day he came again, but this time he had a pizza.

"Sorry," Molly said.

Ben shook his head and put the pizza on her desk. When he'd gone, Kaitlyn peeked around the corner. She watched him saunter across the parking lot and get into his car. When Molly opened the box, Kaitlyn pulled it away from her and took it to her room.

The next day as Ben was coming in, Kaitlyn was passing the communal living area on the way to her room. He had flowers this time, which did catch her eye. She headed straight for him, took the bouquet from his hands, and tossed them in the trash before heading back to her room.

Molly picked them up out of the garbage can and placed them on her desk.

* * *

"May I have some time off for good behavior?" Cameron asked at breakfast.

"What'd you have in mind?" Bill murmured, perusing the morning paper.

"In light of the fact that I've been your virtual shadow since I've been here and haven't really given you a hard time about it . . . "

"What is it you want Cameron?"

"I want to borrow your car and go see my friends."

"Okay."

"I can take the convertible?"

"Yes."

"You realize I'd be leaving the island?"

"Uh huh."

"I might not be back until much later."

"I know."

"But you don't trust me."

"Interesting sales-pitch Cam. You want the car or not?"

"Yeah!" Cameron said, almost laughing.

Bill tossed him the keys, and Cameron stared at them for a moment in disbelief.

"I'm almost afraid to ask if I have a curfew."

"Do you *need* one?"

"No sir," he answered, heading quickly for the door.

"Cam," Bill called out.

"I knew it," he said turning around, as his shoulders sunk.

"Have a good time," Bill said smiling.

"Yeah . . . I will."

"No drinking."

When Cameron closed the front door, Bill chuckled to himself.

"Was that the best idea?" Olivia said, sitting down at the table with a cup of coffee.

"Isn't Iris going to the zoo with your mom and dad today?" he asked, raising his brows.

"Yes," she said smiling.

"Then I'd say that couldn't have worked out better."

* * *

Ben still had no news from Greta but that didn't stop him from going to the children's home yet again to see Kaitlyn. She rolled her eyes when she saw him approach and headed for the hallway as usual.

"Blythe," he called.

She stopped and took a deep breath, turning to look at him.

"Please," he added.

"What is it you want anyway?" she asked. "What are you doing coming here every day?"

He pulled out some workbooks and pencils.

"Something that should have been done a long time ago."

"None of my teachers seem all that concerned, why should I be?" she said, folding her arms.

"Your teachers aren't going to be standing in your place when you get out of here and have nowhere to go and no skills with which to begin life as an adult."

"I'm not going to sit here like some idiot and read, See Dick Run."

"Idiocy isn't characterized by something you don't know how to do. I'd say learning to read at your age would take great courage."

"You really think calling me a chicken is going to make me want to do this?"

"I'm at a loss here Blythe. I have no earthly idea what's going to make you want to do this."

"I curse the day I ever took your bike."

"Many do," he said under his breath. "Now let's start with the basics. Do you know the alphabet?"

"What's that mean? Many do."

"Do you know the alphabet?" he asked again.

"Of course I know the alphabet! I'm not stupid."

"And again . . . it wouldn't make you stupid if you didn't. Not doing something, which may greatly improve your life, now *that* would be stupid."

"I suppose you're going to offer to get me out of trouble again to get what you want?"

"I've already made the call. You can consider the matter closed."

"So this little human relations project is in exchange for finding my brother then?"

"Nope."

"Be straight with me old man. What is it you *do* want?"

"Nothing. I'm hoping you see the wisdom of learning to read without anything else to motivate you."

"Is this court ordered community service?" she asked.

"Nope."

"Lost a bet?"

"No. Can we do this?" he asked.

"So you took care of my court date?"

"Yes."

"And you're going to find Matty whether or not I agree to let you teach me to read?"

"I'm going to try. Yes."

"What's that mean exactly?"

He took an exasperated breath and sat back against the sofa.

"It means I gave you my word that I would try to find your brother, and I'll keep it. I will use every resource at my disposal to bring you two together."

"Why?"

"Because family is important . . . and he's all you have left of it in the world Blythe."

Her eyes filled and she quickly wiped them.

"Not today," she whispered.

"Are you saying that if I come back here tomorrow, you'll do this?" he asked.

She gave a slight nod.

"And the homework too?"

"Don't push it old man," she said, wiping her cheek and left him there.

He put the workbooks back in his bag and smiled to himself.

"Congratulations Mr. Gerard," Molly said, nodding.

"Yes Ma'am."

* * *

Bill sat in the quiet of his office, putting the last touches on the next day's sermon when he heard the front door close. He looked at the clock.

"You're certainly back earlier than I would have expected," he said, when Cameron walked in.

Cameron nodded and plopped down on the couch.

"Things not go well with your friends?" he asked, noticing the kid looked less than happy.

"I have to show you something," Cameron sighed.

"Okay," Bill said, taking off his glasses.

He followed downstairs and out to the garage.

"Were you drinking when you did this?" Bill asked, brushing his hand against the scratches on the side of his convertible.

Cameron said nothing.

"I asked you a question," Bill said, annoyed.

"I haven't had anything to drink."

"So was this an accident? Or was it done out of carelessness?"

"Nothing I say is going to make a difference."

"I don't even get an explanation?" Bill asked. "Fine. Don't ask to borrow my car again anytime soon," he said, leaving Cameron alone in the garage.

* * *

"Are you ready to get to work young lady?" Ben asked.

Kaitlyn sighed and followed Ben to the dining table.

He opened his bag and pulled out alphabet charts and papers with letters outlined in dots for practice.

"Wow, back to basics," she muttered.

"I've found in almost any situation it's best to start at the beginning," he explained.

* * *

As the day stretched toward late afternoon, Ben thought they had done enough. He was pleased that Kaitlyn did, in fact, know the alphabet, though her letter writing would need some work.

"Anything on Matty?" she asked, as Ben put away the workbooks and pencils.

"Not yet."

"So when should I look forward to another of these torture sessions?"

"I think Sunday afternoons will do nicely," Ben said.

She nodded and chewed on her thumbnail.

"See you next week Blythe," he smiled.

* * *

"What's going on today?" Cameron asked Bill, in an effort to break the ghastly silence that had shrouded the breakfast table.

"Today you are going to hang drywall and paint it," Bill said, not looking up from the morning paper.

"Shouldn't there be a *we* in that sentence," Cameron said, winking at Iris.

"No Cameron. *You* were the one who caused over a thousand dollars worth of damage to Olivia's convertible, so there is only a *you* in that sentence."

Bill got up then and put his breakfast plate in the sink. When he left the room Olivia gave Cameron a dry smile.

"Give it time," she said sweetly.

"I have a feeling this is going to be a super-fun day," Cameron said, following Bill out the door.

* * *

Bill worked in silence for the first time since Cameron had met him.

"When you're done painting this room let me know," Bill said. "There are four others."

"Whose place is this?" Cameron asked.

"Not your concern," Bill said, heading for the kitchen.

He watched Bill climb under the sink to install a garbage disposal.

"Where did you learn to do all this stuff anyway?" he asked.

"My father owned a plumbing company while I was growing up. I learned a lot before I left my parent's home."

"Seems pretty unfair of your father to have expected you to be his junior plumber when you were just a kid."

"Yeah well, some kids actually have to work Cameron. Speaking of which, if you don't get in there that paint will dry in two different colors."

"Look, I know you're mad, but for the record, I wasn't the one who scratched up the car."

Bill tossed his wrench onto the kitchen floor and pulled himself out to look Cameron in the eye.

"You were the one to whom I loaned the car. Therefore, *you* were responsible for it, but it seems taking responsibility isn't really your *thing* is it?"

"What does *that* mean?"

"It means, instead of owning responsibility, you'd rather blame someone else. Now get back in that room and work off some the damage you did to my car, because that's what a man would do Cameron—without complaint, without a chip on his shoulder, without another word about it!"

* * *

Ben sat in Greta's waiting room with his cap in his hands until Greta opened the door to her office and waved him in.

"Joshua Deckland," she said, getting right down to business.

"The boy's new name?" Ben asked, raising his eyebrows.

"Yes sir. Adopted by John and Ellen Deckland of Atlanta."

"Georgia?"

"Seems he's lived out there since the adoption."

"Listen, I'd like you to find out some other things, before I even mention this," Ben said, writing her a check.

"Sure thing."

"I'll get a list over to you this week," he promised.

* * *

When lunchtime rolled around Bill poked his head into the room Cameron was painting.

"Nice job," he said, scanning the walls.

"Don't sound so surprised," Cameron said, wrapping his paintbrush in plastic.

"Sandwiches ok?" Bill asked.

"No. A spoiled brat like me only eats steak and lobster."

Bill handed Cameron a sandwich covered in waxed paper.

"Maybe after we finish the job," he chuckled.

* * *

Cameron held Iris over the candle-lit back porch table, so she could place some wild flowers in a vase. When he placed her back on the ground he held up his hand and she slapped her tiny hand against his.

"Great job partner," he said, tousling her head. "Now let's go check on dinner."

By the time Bill and Olivia made it home from running errands, Cameron and Iris had the lights turned low and the back porch set for dinner.

"What smells like heaven?" Olivia asked.

"I helped Tamron make dinner for you and daddy," Iris smiled, taking her mother's hand and pulling her through the living room.

"Since when can you cook?" Bill chuckled, following them to the back porch.

"Oh Bill, I think you'll find that I have many hidden talents," Cameron muttered, lighting the last candle.

"It's only set for two," Olivia said, looking at two plates, a towel covered basket, and a salad in the middle of the table.

"My partner and I are going to walk down to the strip-mall to grab a burger," said Cameron. "The lasagna is in the oven and the rolls are in the basket."

"I picked the flowers," said Iris.

"They're lovely," Olivia said, brushing her fingers through Iris's hair.

Bill eyed Cameron as he sat at the table and Cameron smirked back at him.

"I just thought Olivia might enjoy a nice evening," Cameron said, taking Iris by the hand. "Ready for a burger?" he asked, looking down at her. She looked up at him and nodded her head, furiously.

"Cameron," Bill called to him, as they headed out the door.

"Yeah?"

Bill tossed his keys and Cameron caught them.

9

Light on the Horizon

"Can I ask you a question?" Cameron asked, as Bill pulled into the parking lot of the Saint Raphael Homeless Shelter.

"Shoot."

"Why doesn't Mr. Torres just call on the Vatican for help?"

"Because Saint Raphael isn't affiliated with the Catholic Church," Bill explained.

"I suppose the *saint* part threw me."

"Good morning," John said, meeting them at the door.

Cameron noticed Jack playing in the corner with his mother nearby. He followed Bill into John's office, but kept an eye on Jack.

"How are we looking?" Bill asked when they sat down.

"Thanks to LWC we just might make it to Christmas," John smiled.

"It's too bad people aren't in a giving mood in July like they are in December," Bill remarked, scanning the penciled figures in John's notebook.

"What is LWC?" Cameron asked.

"It's my church," Bill said and excused himself.

"I figured you must be one of his congregants," John said.

"No."

"Where do you go to church?" John asked.

"I don't. Can you tell me why that little boy and his mother are back here?" Cameron asked, pointing to Jack.

"The Robinson's?" John said. "Thank God we had space for them once they spelled."

"Spelled?" Cameron asked.

John furrowed his brow at the kid.

"Okay Cam, we should get to work. We have a lot to do here today before we head back to the island," Bill said, poking his head into John's office.

Bill ripped the duct-tape from the broken window and brushed away the glass.

"I should have realized LWC stood for Living Word Church," Cameron said, helping brush away the rest of the glass.

"That's all right," Bill chuckled. "Let's get the new pane over here."

"Why don't they get a handyman?" Cameron asked, looking around.

"They did," Bill said, with a box cutter between his teeth. "And today they got two for the price of one."

"Mr. Torres said the Robinson's *spelled*. What does that mean?"

"The shelter only has twenty-five beds available at a time," Bill explained.

"So?"

"So, that means a person, or a family, can only stay here for a limited time. After that they have to be gone for at least two weeks before they can come back. A spell."

"Where do they go when they leave here?" Cameron asked, looking over at Jack.

"Some go to stay with family, or to another shelter, if they're lucky."

"And the others?"

Bill followed Cameron's eyes to Jack.

"They came here to eat in the day, but it's very likely that Jack and Nora slept in doorways or maybe a restroom at the bus terminal before they came back here."

Cameron took a deep breath as he looked around.

Bill could see the change in Cameron's demeanor, but he had no idea what was going on inside the kid. As he played the memory of meeting Jack and Emanuel, something in him was shifting, changing. He wondered where all the do-gooders were when these kids needed them. Losing his father had been difficult and he found himself wishing Warren were still around so that he could share these tragedies with him. His mother and father were no strangers to helping the less fortunate, but he'd never seen anything as hands-on as he did now working with Bill. As he imagined what it would be like to sleep in a public restroom without a bed or a kitchen, he felt a sudden urgency to make sure these people were okay. Cameron found himself wondering if there was anything more he could do than to fix windows as Bill snapped him from his thoughts.

"Okay," Bill said, examining the window. "That should do."

The kid followed him to one of the bathrooms, where Bill taught him how to snake out a toilet. They replaced the condenser fan in the kitchen refrigerator. When they were finished with that, Cameron followed Bill up a ladder to the roof where they patched a leak.

* * *

"Good day's work," Bill said. "I can't wait to see what Liv's got going for dinner."

Cameron's growling stomach seemed to be overshadowed by the ache in his heart. John thanked him and when he reached for the kid's hand, Cameron shook it with a firm grasp. He had discovered an awful truth about manhood that day. For Cameron, it seemed to be a genuine conflict between the backbreaking work he had done, and the recognition that he was completely powerless to help these people.

* * *

Ben kneeled at his bedside and thanked God for helping him find Matthew Blythe. He prayed for the following year's Consuming Fire weekend. The new bike would do nicely in lending a hand to make it happen and he asked God for protection in setting the traps to bait the new fish. Before he finished, he paused.

"God please take the thorn from my side, whenever you see fit."

He wasn't sure whether or not he could bring himself to say anything more about Ray. He trusted that God had a better understanding of his heart than he did himself, so he simply left it at that.

* * *

Cameron was jolted awake but he couldn't recall the dream that had woken him. As his pulse slowed he rolled over to see what time it was. Four in the morning was too early to get up even though he was wide-awake. He switched on the little lamp beside the sofa bed and looked over at the Bible on Bill's desk.

* * *

Kaitlyn wasn't feeling up to a lesson. She'd have preferred to stay in her room sketching. When Ben showed up he wasn't carrying his bag. She searched his eyes.

"An investigator has found Matthew."

"Matty?" she whispered. "Is he all right?"

"Yes. It seems he was adopted soon after the accident."

"Where is he? Can I see him?"

"Let's sit down," Ben said, motioning toward the table. "There are some things you should know."

"What things?"

"He lives in Georgia."

"I don't mind going all the way to Georgia to meet him."

"Hold on a minute," Ben said, holding up his hands. "There's more. It was a closed adoption. He may not even know about you."

"So? It'll be the surprise of his life. Hey kid, you have a sister."

"Is that something you really want to take into your own hands?"

"Why shouldn't I?"

"Because it seems to me that you love your brother."

"That's exactly why I want him to know who I am. What is the matter with you?" she asked. "You tell me that you're going to find my brother, and now you won't let me see him?"

"No one said you couldn't see him. All I'm saying is, let's do this slowly and do it right, so you end up with a relationship with him. If we handle this the wrong way it might scare off his adoptive parents."

"I don't give a rip about his adoptive parents."

"But he *does. He* does."

"Where do you get off telling me *we're* going to handle this? There is no we. This is between Matty and me. This has nothing to do with you."

"I wish you would listen to me," Ben pleaded. "This situation calls for delicacy, and I'm afraid that's something you're a bit short on Blythe."

"I'd say I've listened enough. Thank you very much for finding Matty. Now give me his number and I'll deal with this myself."

Ben handed her a piece of paper and let out a sigh.

"If you do this, there's a good chance you're going to lose him, at least for a good long while."

She pulled the paper from his hands and looked at it. She saw the name and knew immediately it did not say Matthew. She sounded it out.

"Joshua Deck . . . Deckland?"

"A whole new name and a whole new life," said Ben, cautioning her.

* * *

Cameron offered to stay in the car while Bill checked on one of his congregants at a nearby apartment building.

"You can come along. It might be a while."

"Who lives here anyway?" Cameron asked, eyeing the run-down building.

"Remember the couple who came to dinner after you'd first arrived?"

"Sort of. She goes to church, he doesn't?"

"The Reynolds," Bill said nodding. "It seems he's moved out of the house and in here. He agreed to talk to me."

"So you're going to try to get him to come to church and save his marriage?"

"One hurdle at a time," Bill said sighing.

When Dave Reynolds opened the door, the place smelled like an old bar.

"Come on in preacher," he said, tucking in his shirt.

Cameron gave the guy a dry smile and followed Bill into the apartment, which was just one big room with an adjoining bathroom.

"An efficiency is all I could afford," Dave stammered. "Here have a seat." He offered them each a folding chair. "Sorry about the smell," he added, reaching for a can of air freshener under his sink.

Once the layer of cheap pine mist hit the air and filled his lungs, Cameron found himself longing for the previous odor.

"I have a Bible around here somewhere," Dave said, rummaging through the kitchen drawers and scurrying a bit to clean up as he searched.

"That's okay," Bill said. "Why don't we just talk?"

"Can I get you or your son something to drink?" he asked, opening the fridge.

"I'm fine. Cameron?" Bill asked, looking at him.

Cameron shook his head. This guy was so fidgety that Cameron had become too distracted to even correct him about thinking Bill was his father.

"I'm sorry I don't have much food," Dave said. "I can make you guys some toast."

"You know what, I'd love a cigarette if you have one," Bill said.

Dave raised his eyebrows at Bill and shook his head.

"Yeah . . . sure," he stammered. "Didn't know you guys were allowed to smoke."

Cameron watched in amazement as the guy handed Bill a cigarette and then lit it for him. He lit one for himself and then stuffed the lighter back in his pocket and finally took a seat.

"Sorry I haven't been to church," he started.

"That's okay Dave," Bill assured him. "Tell me what's going on with you and Amanda."

"A couple of weeks ago I lost my job," he explained. "He looked down at the floor and spun his wedding band around his finger a few times. "Right after that I got pulled over and . . . ended up losing my license. Then she kicked me out."

"Have you found work yet?" Bill asked, taking a drag from his cigarette.

Dave shook his head.

"You do cabinetry work right?"

"Damn good at it too— sorry. Good at it."

"A friend of mine may have work. If you'd like, I'll give him your number and maybe he can throw a little your way."

"That'd be great!" Dave said. "Listen, I was planning to come to church on Sunday."

"You like the Dolphins?" Bill smiled, pointing to the furry blanket on the bed decorated with the team's insignia.

"Yes sir. That's my team."

"I'm a Viking's fan myself," Bill smiled.

After a short chat about football, Bill shook Dave's hand and they left.

"How on earth is talking football with some guy going to put his marriage back together?" Cameron asked, as they drove away.

"Did you think I was going to be able to fix his marriage as we sat there?"

"I don't know. I guess I thought this guy's wife wanted you to get him to come to church."

"She does."

"When he offered to come you didn't even take him up on it."

"It wasn't a real offer. Dave was telling me what he thought I wanted to hear."

"You don't want him to come to your church?"

"Of course I do."

"The more people that are there, the more you collect right?"

"Sure," Bill said.

"So, you probably helped him find work. Why wouldn't you take him up on his offer to give a little back?"

"You're suggesting I use his current situation to manipulate him into attending church regularly?"

"I don't get you. Isn't that what you believe? That if a person goes to church and reads their Bible, life will turn out better?"

"Right now, Dave's biggest problem is not a lack of church services. Do I think he'd be better off coming and hearing the Gospel? Of course, but that has to come from him. Right now he needs work, so he can eat, and perhaps when Amanda sees that he's serious about keeping a job, she'll give him another chance."

"Since when do you smoke?" Cameron asked.

"I don't. It was an easy way for him to take me from the pedestal he had me on and talk to me like a friend, instead of someone who's going to check up on him and report back to his wife. Now let's stop somewhere for lunch so I can get this horrible taste out of my mouth."

* * *

Kaitlyn trembled as she held the phone to her ear. By the third ring, her mouth had become so dry she found that she could no longer swallow. She had waited until evening to call, in the hopes that her brother might answer.

"Hello."

It was the voice of a young boy. She squeezed the paper in her hand and tried to muster up some courage.

"Hello?" he repeated.

"Are you happy with your cable service?" she asked.

"I don't know. Mom! Some lady wants to know if we're happy with our cable."

Kaitlyn's eyes filled at the sound of his voice and then his mother got on the line.

"Hello. Hello?" she said.

"Sorry, wrong number," Kaitlyn muttered, hanging up.

* * *

"So, you actually believe God made the earth?" Cameron asked Bill.

"The heavens, the earth, and all that is in them.," Bill said.

"So he made two people, put them in a garden, put a tree there that looked great, told them not to eat anything from it, and then punished them when they did?"

"Sounds like someone's been reading my Bible."

"These stories don't seem a little far-fetched to you?"

"Was that a rhetorical question Cameron?"

"No. I meant it genuinely. You seem a little too smart to believe this stuff."

"There's a compliment in there somewhere," Bill said with a chuckle.

"That *was* a compliment."

"What seems far-fetched to you?"

"Where do I begin?" Cameron said. "How about making a person from dirt? Why wouldn't God just speak people into existence like it says he did with light, and the earth, and the stars?"

"Well, I can't really tell you *why* God chose to do it that way, but what I can tell you is that scientists have told us that we are basically made up of the same composition as the earth, and that cannot be a coincidence."

"Exactly," Cameron said. "We are basically made up of the earth's composition because we evolved from the earth."

"You believe the composition of our bodies disproves the Bible, while I see it the other way around. The Bible simply states it as a fact. Scientific evidence concluded years after the Bible had been written what the writer of that book already knew. Either that, or it was one heck of a guess."

"I just can't wrap my head around some being having created all this," Cameron said, waving his arms.

"The human body is more complex than any machine on earth, and yet you're proposing that it happened without any conscious thought or planning."

"It comes down to this Bill. You claim God created the world, and that he loves us. When I look around all I see is unhappiness. How could a God of love allow that?"

"Do you honestly believe your mother loves you Cameron?"

"Of course."

"And yet, she sent you away, thereby causing you to be unhappy."

"She's just worried about my future. She was doing what she thought she had to do."

"So even though you don't understand the reason for her decision to send you away, you choose to believe that her reason for doing it was love?"

"I suppose."

"I think you just answered your own question."

* * *

Kaitlyn sat at the dining table, pencil in hand, awaiting Ben's arrival.

"Afternoon Blythe," he said, surprised.

"Let's do this."

As Kaitlyn traced letters and sounded out words phonetically, Ben realized her reading was far better than he'd first thought.

"It seems like maybe you've been holding out on me," he smirked, putting away the workbooks.

"Can I hang on to those?" she asked, pointing to the workbooks.

"Of course."

"I called my brother, not that it's any of your business."

"Oh?"

"Let's just suppose for a minute that I want your help."

"Do you?"

"Don't push it old man."

"What would you like me to do?" Ben asked.

"Arrange it so I can see Matty."

"That'll take some thought."

"Well, I guess I'm in luck then . . . seems like all you *do* is think."

* * *

After a long night of fishing, Ben held his walkie-talkie to his mouth.

"Not much going on tonight Sheriff. Heading home."

"I don't know whether to be relieved or disappointed," Logan said back.

Ben held on to the walkie-talkie for a moment and nodded, then hung it up on his dash. He hadn't caught one fish for the next Consuming Fire weekend, but it was early yet. He tossed his remaining coffee out the truck window and pushed the bike back up the ramp. As he tied it down for the ride home he thought about Kaitlyn. Maybe she was the reason he kept coming up empty on his recent fishing expeditions. He had a feeling he knew what he should do.

When Ben got home, he looked around the house. He had lived a solitary life for so long that there was hardly any evidence that Rosie had lived there. He brushed his hands against the plastic flowers in the vase on the dining room table. He never even ate in there anymore. He smoothed the doily that Rosie had placed beneath the vase as his brain conjured the memory of a thousand dinners with her at that very table. He could still see her feeding Ray in his highchair and smiled at the thought of it. The memory of the night Ray died came on so suddenly it startled him. He squeezed his eyes shut tight and then jumped when Caesar hopped up in his lap, reminding him that he hadn't had dinner.

"Suppose you're hungry," he said, brushing his fingers over the cat's head. Roofus whined from his corner on the carpet in the foyer. "You too? Okay, let's eat."

After the three of them had eaten, Ben picked up the phone and booked himself a flight.

* * *

Angela Stowe had forgotten that Farrow Island was so lovely. She hadn't seen Cameron since he packed up to go and stay at Bill and Olivia's place, though he had called a few times. She didn't realize how much she'd missed him, until she pulled up to the house and saw him standing outside with his hands stuffed in his pockets. He smiled at her, and she couldn't help but notice how much he looked like Warren.

"Hi," he said, offering her his hand when she opened the car door.

She tilted her head to look at her son, realizing something about his appearance had changed, though she couldn't quite put her finger on what that might be.

"I'm so glad you came."

"Me too," she agreed.

"C'mon in," Cameron said. "You've got to meet Olivia and Iris."

"Hello again Angela," Bill said, as he offered her his hand.

"Mom, this is Olivia," Cameron said, introducing them. "And this little girl pretending to be part of her mom's leg, is Iris."

"Hi there," Angela said, bending down to meet Iris's eyes.

Iris stayed hidden behind Olivia's legs until Bill lifted her and put her in her chair at the table.

"Mom, can I get you something to drink?" Cameron asked.

"Is that Chicken Marsala I smell?" Angela asked her son.

"Yep."

"Cameron always loved to cook. Warren and I were just amazed at this little kid making all these fancy dishes. It's been a while since you cooked for me," she said, taking a seat at the table.

"Well, I did have help," he said, winking at Iris.

She smiled back at him and kicked her legs under the table.

"She's beautiful," Angela said. "We were always sorry we didn't have at least one more."

"Sometimes one's plenty," Bill laughed, looking at Cameron.

"Sounds like your daddy doesn't want any dinner, doesn't it?" Cameron said, and Iris shook her head and giggled.

Over dinner Cameron told Angela all about Saint Raphael and little Jack. She was amazed at the change in him. She wondered if the time had come to bring him home. When she suggested it over dessert, she was surprised by his reaction.

"Bill and I have a project we're working on right now, but maybe in a few weeks," he said.

"Cameron, if you'd like to go back home, I can finish the addition myself," Bill insisted. "We've been working on a new school-room at the church," he explained.

"Cameron goes to church?" Angela asked, narrowing her brow.

"No," he said quickly. "But that doesn't stop Bill from telling me Bible stories."

"Warren and I were never what you'd call *religious*," she said, reaching for her coffee.

"Religion is a dirty word at our house," Cameron said with a chuckle. "In case you didn't pick up on my mother's tone."

"Cameron, that's not true," she said, clearing her throat.

"Actually, it *is* true, but there are a lot of things you and dad never stopped to consider."

She took a deep breath and looked around the dining room.

"So did you decorate the house or did you have someone come in and do it?" Angela asked. "I love the style."

"Notice the swift change in subject matter," Cameron smirked. "Actually, I was thinking I might go to church this Sunday," he added, looking at Bill.

"I was thinking I might bring you home," his mother said, taking another sip of her coffee.

"I told you I can't leave now. Bill and I still have work to do."

"Iris, will you help me clear the dinner table?" Olivia asked.

"I'll get it," Cameron said, standing up.

"Cameron, why don't you let us clean up? Go spend some time with your mother," Bill suggested.

Cameron looked at Bill, fearing they'd made him and Olivia uncomfortable.

"Walk?" he said to his mother.

* * *

"I'm glad you like these people Cameron," Angela said. "I just think it's time to come home now."

"I'll be home soon," he assured her.

"Do you remember coming out here with your dad and me?" she asked, looking around the island as they walked.

"Not really."

"I suppose you were too young to remember."

"Mom listen, there's something I'd like to do."

"What is it?"

"I'd like to bust my trust-fund a little early."

"How early?"

"Eighteen."

"Why can't you wait until your twenty-five? Your father and I figured that would be a perfect age to start paying off your education. You'll have two of your degree's by then and you'll likely just be starting out."

"I know you think at eighteen a kid is too young to handle that kind of money—that I'd blow it on something stupid. I'm not going to do that."

"What do you want it for?"

He looked at her and tilted his head.

"You know that shelter I told you about over dinner?"

"Cameron, you can't help everyone."

"But I *can* help those people."

"I think it's terrific that you've begun to notice the world around you, I really do, but Cameron that money is for your future."

"Suppose helping people becomes my future instead?"

"You're young, I get it. You think you can save the world, but you have to understand that there is a reason those people ended up in the situation that they're in. I'm not trying to be heartless."

"It just comes naturally then?"

She let out an exasperated sigh.

"You're not touching that money, and one day you'll be glad, believe me."

"So you're saying, my degrees are more important than several people having a better quality of life?"

"Cameron, stop and think for a moment. Do you really want to join the homeless and the downtrodden? What good would *that* do? With an education you could be as good a lawyer one day as your father was. After you've jumped *that* hurdle, help whomever you want. You are welcome to do all the pro-bono work your heart desires, if you still want to."

"If I still *want* to?"

"Quite often, after a few years out in the real world, people find that their altruistic idealism wears off."

"What do you know about the *real* world?" Cameron sneered. "You married dad right out of high school. You've never had to work a day in your life. You've never wanted for anything. You've never had less than a few hundred thousand dollars in your account to do with as you please. What do you know about not having shoes for your child, or sleeping in doorways?"

"Nothing. I know nothing about ending up that way, for a good reason Cameron."

"Oh, that's right. You were smart enough to have married well," he snapped.

"That's not what I meant, and you know it. I would have been fine, even if I'd never met your father."

"Like Aunt Rocky?"

"It's not my fault that she decided on a nothing life."

"Yeah well, I guess she wasn't pretty enough to get a young lawyer to fall in love with her like you were Mom."

"Has it occurred to you that I went back to school to get my own degree?"

"A lot of good it's done you."

"Very well, has it occurred to you that I have raised money for the homeless?"

"Are you talking about those tax-deductible, ritzy fundraisers, you throw now and then to make yourself feel better?"

"So according to you, unless a person has eaten out of a dumpster they haven't experienced real life? Real pain? Living here with these people for a couple of months hasn't made you some kind of savior to the world Cameron."

"Living your cushy, little, suburban life, hasn't made *you* one either."

"I'm not so sure this place is good for you."

"You just hate not being able to control me."

"That's not true," she insisted.

"Of course it is. You sent me here because I was out of control. Now I have some direction, but because I no longer want to be the little snob you were hoping for, you're not happy with this either."

"Is that what they're feeding you? That we're snobs because our family has a little more than most people? Your father worked long and hard to get us into a good position."

"First of all, they're not feeding me anything. Unlike you, Bill and Olivia are genuinely concerned for the welfare of others. Second of all, our family has a *lot* more than most people."

"This conversation's going nowhere. I want you to get your things together and come home with me."

"I'll be home after Bill and I have finished the new addition. Oh, and I *will* find a way to get the money for the shelter. I hope you enjoyed dinner."

Bill pushed the blinds aside and watched Angela drive away as Cameron made his way into the house.

"Your mother didn't say goodbye. Was she upset?"

"She'll get over it."

10

In the Making

"Your mother was pretty upset when she left last night," Bill said to Cameron as they worked.

"Maybe that's a good thing."

"Were you serious about coming to church on Sunday?"

"Don't get excited Bill, I'm not converting, just curious."

"It's not your conversion that concerns me."

"Yeah? What concerns you about my coming to church then? Is curiosity not a good enough reason to show up?"

"It felt a lot like you were saying it just to annoy your mother. And *that* would be a terrible reason to do something."

"Relax, I meant what I said. My mother being shaken up by it . . . well that's just a perk."

Bill stopped then and put down his hammer.

"Cameron, you know how they tell you to turn into a skid?"

"Is this about the car again?"

"No. This is about you over-correcting in your life. While I'm delighted to see that you've found something to be passionate about, I'd hate to see you alienate your mother. You're all she has left."

Cameron tossed the measuring tape in his hand to the ground and shook his head.

"My mother has everything. She's selfish and stubborn. Do you want to know what our fight was about last night?"

"Only if you'd like to share it with me."

"I have more money than I need. I'd like to use it to help Saint Raphael keep its doors open. I'd like to make it bigger so kids like Jack and Emanuel don't have to sleep on the streets. My mother is more concerned that I hang on to my money so I can pay for a bunch of fancy degrees, which will ensure my entry into the same country-club life she has."

"Saving money for college is something any decent parent would want for their kid."

"That's pretty funny, coming from a guy who emptied his savings account to help that same shelter."

"I didn't use Iris's college money to do it."

"Are you saying if you had a choice between Iris attending some Ivy League school, and helping a bunch of people get on their feet, you don't know what you would do? I've only known you a few months and *I* know what you would do."

"I would make sure Iris had an education."

"No one said I'm not going to college. So I go to a state school instead. Is there something wrong with that?"

"I don't know, I mean a lot of people would give their right arm to have graduated from a top-notch university verses a state school."

"I can still get a decent degree from a local school."

"Yeah but, Harvard Law degree, has a nice ring to it, doesn't it?"

* * *

"Can I help you?" Ellen Deckland said to Ben, when she opened the door to find him standing on her porch.

"I hope so. My name is Ben Gerard."

Nothing he'd rehearsed in his mind sounded appropriate now that they were face to face.

"And?"

"I understand that your son Joshua was adopted."

"Who told you that?"

"A private investigator."

"Who hired a private investigator? Are we under surveillance? We haven't done anything wrong. We—"

"Hold on a minute," Ben said, putting up his hands. "You're not in any trouble. It's nothing like that."

"Then what is this about?"

"May I please come in? This conversation is a little personal for the front porch."

"I'd prefer it if you stayed out here."

"Very well. At the time of the death of your son's natural parents, were you aware that they had another child?"

"What about her?" Ellen asked.

"You know about Kaitlyn?"

"Yes. We did a little investigating of our own."

"What do you know about her?"

"That she's nothing but trouble. We considered taking them both at first, but she was handful even then."

"She was five when her parents died," Ben pointed out.

"We only wanted an infant at the time. We thought maybe once Joshua settled in we would take her too, but then as he got older we worried about her influence on him. We also worried that she might tell him he was adopted."

"Do you plan to tell him at some point?"

"Once he's an adult and can handle it, we'll let him know."

"Eight more years?" Ben asked.

"At least. It's not like we're setting a date to give him that news."

"What about Kaitlyn's desire to see him?"

"She's not our responsibility."

"She just wants to know her family."

"Are you telling me she remembers Joshua?"

"Of course. She was five at the time of their parents' death."

"*We* are Joshie's parents."

"Ma'am . . . Mrs. Deckland, your son is all she has in the world. What harm would there be in letting them meet?"

"Absolutely not. We'll decide when and how to tell Joshie. If he wants to get to know her someday, that will up to him. Now I'd appreciate it if you would be on your way."

"Here is my number," Ben said, handing her a slip of paper. "Please call me if you change your mind."

"I won't," she assured him, with her arms still folded.

"Will you at least talk it over with your husband?"

She stared at him, but said nothing.

"You can throw my number away if you want to, but please take it and just think about it."

She took the number from him and stared at it for a moment.

"There is a reason we chose a *closed* adoption. What you are asking me to do is unthinkable."

"What I'm asking, is for you to consider a little girl, whose life was destroyed through no fault of her own. She has one hope in the world; a brother she desperately wants to know."

* * *

Cameron took his seat at the breakfast table and shuffled through what was left of the newspaper.

"We want to talk to you," Olivia said.

"Whatever it is . . . it wasn't me," he joked.

"It wasn't me," Iris mimicked.

Cameron laughed. He had never had the luxury of blame sharing with a sibling, and was amused at how naturally it seemed to evolve in the hierarchy of a family.

"What is it?" he asked, still grinning.

"Bill and I think perhaps it's time for you to go home," Olivia said softly.

"But there are still a few weeks left of summer. If I've overstayed my welcome—"

"No. We were afraid you might think that," Bill said. "Nothing could be less true."

"We all love having you here Cameron," Olivia said. "Especially Iris."

"Then why do you want me to leave early?" he asked.

"We don't *want* you to leave," Bill said. "We just feel like your mother needs you now."

"Did she call you?" he asked, looking at Olivia.

"No sweetheart."

"Is this about the other night?" he asked.

"Partly," Bill said.

"Don't let my argument with her bother you. We argue all the time. Even when my father was alive."

Bill and Olivia looked at each other and Cameron could tell they had already decided he was leaving before they'd told him.

"So once again, I don't get a say in what happens to me? This is getting pretty old."

"Stop it," Bill said. "You're not that kid anymore."

"When do you want me to leave?" he asked, folding the newspaper he'd been skimming.

"The damage on the car has been fixed, but it seems Olivia doesn't want it anymore. So we were thinking we would go out today and buy a new one, and you can leave after that."

"You need my help getting a deal at the car lot?" Cameron asked.

"No. We're giving you the convertible."

"What? Why? All I've done is cause you trouble and cost you money. You could trade it in and get a better deal on a new car."

"Again, quite a sales-pitch Cam. You want the car or not?"

"I want to know why you're giving me a car? Is it because you feel guilty about giving me the boot?"

"No. We knew we'd be giving you the boot soon anyway," Bill said, grinning.

"This makes no sense. You know very well that my mother can afford to buy me a brand new car."

"Yes, and you retain that option," Bill said. "If you don't want it, you certainly don't have to take it."

"I just want to know why," Cameron said, looking at Olivia.

"Because we love you Cameron, and we want to give you a gift."

* * *

Ben had no idea what he'd say to Kaitlyn. When he arrived at the children's home she was already at the table studying.

"Your writing is coming along very well," Ben said, looking over her shoulder.

"Not bad, if I do say so myself," she grinned, sitting back in her chair.

"You should do much better this school year."

"Yeah well, I'm only doing it for Matty."

"What do you mean?"

"I don't want to be the girl who can't even read and write as well as her ten-year-old brother."

"I see. I'd like you to take an aptitude test this year," Ben said, figuring she would argue.

"What's that?"

"It's a test designed to figure out what you should be aiming for with your life."

"Never really thought about it," she admitted.

"Well Blythe, the time has come to think about it. What do you enjoy doing?"

"Enjoy? What's *that* got to do with making money?"

"A lot of people make a living doing something they enjoy."

"There isn't a whole lot of money in the things I like doing," she assured him.

"Well, stealing aside, you might be surprised."

"I'm waiting to hear about my brother."

"I've spoken to your brother's adoptive mother," he said, narrowing his eyes at her.

As she studied the look on his face, her smile faded.

"They don't want me to talk to him, do they?"

"Not now, no."

"Then when?"

"Listen Blythe—"

"Get out," she whispered.

"If we just keep working—"

"I said, get out! And take these with you!"

She tossed the workbooks at him and ran to her room.

"I'm sorry," Molly said, coming around to help him.

"She's lost a lot," Ben said. "I'll give it some time."

* * *

Cameron walked down the stairs and set his bag on the kitchen floor. He wasn't sure what to say to Bill and Olivia.

"Where are you going Tamron?" Iris said, when she saw his bag.

"I've got to go, squirt."

"I want to go with Tamron," she said, running to him.

He caught her in his arms and picked her up.

"I'll make you a deal. You stay here with Mommy and Daddy and I'll visit you as often as I can, okay?"

"No," she said. "You stay too."

"I need you to watch your dad while I'm gone. Make sure he does what your mom tells him."

"Everyone listens to Mommy," Iris said.

"That's right," Cameron said, putting her down.

Olivia put her arms around him and kissed his cheek.

"We're here if you need us," she said, holding his face and looking into his eyes. She smiled at him and took Iris by the hand. "Ready for bath time?" she asked, heading to the bathroom.

Bill handed him the keys to the convertible as Cameron picked up his bag. He didn't realize how much he was going to miss the kid until they were heading out to the driveway to say goodbye.

"I'd have come out to church, even if you hadn't given me the car," Cameron smirked, tossing his bag on to the passenger's seat.

"I'd have given you the car, even if you hadn't promised to come out to church," said Bill shrugging.

Cameron nodded and grinned. When he put out his hand, Bill reached around his neck and pulled him into a hug instead.

"I'm proud of you Cam," he said, patting his back.

A few months ago, those words would have fallen on deaf ears, now they were like a balm to the kid. Bill waved at him as Cameron drove away.

* * *

When Ben's phone rang, he wasn't very surprised. He suspected it was only a matter of time until Kaitlyn tried to find her brother. He wasn't expecting the call to be from her, however. He thought one of these nights he'd get a call from Logan or maybe even Molly Bivens.

"Yeah, this is Ben."

"Ben?" she sounded terrified. He heard a scuffle on the other end of the line.

"Blythe? Blythe? Is that you?"

"This is Greg Handleman. I have a little girl here who has broken into my house. If she hadn't been so young I'd have called the police by now. She says you're her only relative. If you're not here to pick her up within the hour, she's going to jail."

Ben clicked the lamp on his bedside and grabbed a pencil.

"Give me your address, I'll be there as soon as possible," he promised.

When the man rattled off the address Ben realized it would take at least that long to drive there.

"I'm all the way out in Polk County," Ben explained. "Please give me some time to get there."

"You have an hour," said Greg, hanging up.

Ben rushed to get dressed and headed out the door. He thought about calling Logan to give him a heads-up, but the address was out of his jurisdiction. He figured he could call Logan if he got there and saw that he needed him. Ben couldn't get the sound of Kaitlyn's voice out of his head. In the short time that he'd known her, he couldn't recall her ever having been afraid of anything, not even when he'd caught her stealing his bike. When he pulled up to the old house, he saw the curtains in the living room window yank back. Ben knocked on the door and heard Greg yell out that he could come in. When he walked in, Ben saw that Greg had Kaitlyn sitting in a chair in the corner of the room at gunpoint.

"Easy," Ben said, holding out his hands. "Let's not have that thing out where it could hurt someone."

"*This* is your only living relative?" Greg asked laughing.

"I was the only one she could call," Ben said, with his hands still in front of him.

"You two working together? This some kind of a scam you got going?" Greg said, waving the gun from Ben to Kaitlyn and back again.

Ben shook his head and looked at Kaitlyn.

"Get up slowly and go get in the truck Blythe," Ben told her.

"What's an old black man doing with a teenage thief?" Greg asked, as she slowly made her way past them.

"We don't want any trouble with you," Ben said. "She's just a scared kid. She was probably just looking for something to eat."

"Yeah, I'm sure she's an honor student," Greg said, still pointing the gun at Ben. "She knocked out the window on my back door and for all I know you told her to do it."

"I'll pay for whatever damage she's done," Ben said, reaching for his billfold. As he reached inside his jacket pocket, a nearby car backfired and Greg squeezed the trigger before he could even think about what was happening. Kaitlyn heard the shot and saw Ben go down on his knees in the doorway. By the time she got to him, Ben had already lost consciousness.

"What did you do?" she said looking up at Greg. "Why did you shoot him?"

"I thought he had a gun!" Greg yelled. "I thought he sent you here to rob me." He looked back and forth between them, still holding the gun.

"Put that thing away before you shoot me too!" she yelled. "Call an ambulance! What are you waiting for?"

Greg stood there weighing his options and she realized he wasn't going to call for help.

"Help me get him into the truck."

Kaitlyn pulled Ben from under his arms and dragged him to his truck.

As Greg stood dumbfounded at the end of the driveway, Kaitlyn screeched off toward the highway with Ben thrown across the passenger seat. She followed signs to the nearest hospital and pulled into the emergency roundabout.

"Help me!" she yelled, as the sliding doors opened. She ran around the truck and opened the door. Ben opened his eyes and looked at her for a moment before two EMT's pulled him from the seat and placed him on a gurney.

* * *

Kaitlyn kept her distance, watching policeman come and go from the hospital. She had pulled Ben's truck around to general parking and found some change in the ashtray. She was careful to use a different hospital entrance to look for a vending machine. She hadn't eaten in at least a day and a half. She settled into a waiting room chair and finished off two bags of potato chips and a can of root beer before nodding off. She was awakened by an announcement over the loud speaker, calling a doctor to surgery. She flinched and looked around wondering how long she had been asleep. Surely the night staff had gone by now. She thought maybe it would be safe to sneak back around to the emergency room and try to find Ben. She walked up and down the halls, figuring by now they had to have admitted him. She saw a policeman sitting outside a room. She waited until she saw him walk away and darted inside.

"Figures the one person in the world who cares anything about me would get shot," she muttered.

"Blythe?" he said, opening his eyes.

"Didn't mean to wake you. You okay?" she asked.

"Where did you go?"

"I waited on the other side of the hospital. Too many cops around."

"What happened?" he asked, looking around the room.

"That lunatic shot you."

"You broke into his house."

"Yeah well, I'd say that was still an overreaction. Someone wound up that tight shouldn't own a gun."

Kaitlyn heard a scuffle outside the door and ran into the bathroom.

"He's awake," she heard the officer say as he came into Ben's room.

"Mr. Gerard, I'm officer Vantas. We're going to need you to help us make a report," he said to Ben.

"Right now?" Ben asked.

"While it's still fresh is the best time."

Ben glanced at the bathroom door and nodded.

"Can we make this quick? I'm so tired."

"How did you get to the hospital? The emergency room staff said a young woman brought you here in a truck, but by the time they got you inside, she was gone."

"I have no idea how I got here," Ben lied. "I think I must have been unconscious at the time."

"Well, who shot you?"

"I don't know."

"The angle of the shot tells us that you were face to face with the assailant, and at close range, so surely you got a look at them."

"I don't know who he was."

"Can you describe him?" Vantas asked.

"It all happened so fast."

"Can you tell me *where* it happened?"

"Out on Route 50 somewhere."

"Somewhere? *Where* on Route 50? And what were you doing there?"

"I had trouble sleeping. Got up around midnight to go for a drive. The truck started giving me some trouble so I pulled over. I waved someone down to call for help and he robbed me. He must have also been the one who shot me."

"You were robbed?"

"Yes sir."

"But the hospital staff found your wallet on your person when you came in."

"Maybe the shooter forgot to take it in the scuffle."

"Forgive me, Mr. Gerard, but it's highly unlikely that a thief would go through the trouble of shooting you and then leave the scene without the things he came for. Did you get a look at him?"

"I told you, it happened so fast, and it was dark."

"Where is your truck now?"

"It must have been stolen."

"Who was the girl who brought you here? Was it *your* truck she brought you in?"

"I have no recollection of her at all. She must have found me on the side of the road and taken me to the hospital."

"So, let me get this straight," Vantas said. "You were driving down Route 50 some time after midnight when your truck began to show signs of trouble. You pulled over and flagged someone down for help, whom you cannot identify, and he shot you, but didn't rob you. He likely took your truck and then a Good Samaritan, a young woman, came by and drove you to the hospital in a truck which may or may not have been yours, leaving before she could be identified."

"I don't think the man meant to shoot me."

"How do you know *that*?"

"I sort of remember his being surprised by the whole thing."

"Even though you couldn't see him?"

"He kind of made a noise when the gun went off like it was an accident."

"Well, this has got to be the strangest robbery I've ever reported. We can't even get an I.D. on the gun, because the bullet went straight through your hip and clean out the other side."

There was a knock at the door then and Logan walked in.

"Ben, you okay?" Logan asked.

"Will, I'm fine. I don't really remember what happened. I'm afraid I haven't been much help to this officer."

"Sheriff Will Logan, Polk County," Will said to the reporting officer.

"Officer Vantas," he said back to him. "You know this man?"

"Yes," Will said, smiling at Ben. "We go back a lot of years."

"Well, maybe you can get more details from him. I'm going to call this in and see if we can get somebody out to Route 50 to find any other evidence of this mess."

"What happened?" Will said, once Vantas left the room.

"It was an accident Will, it really was. Listen, I need you to find my truck and dump it off of Route 50 somewhere out by the border of Polk and Long Gate."

"You're joking."

"Will. Please."

Logan shook his head and chuckled.

"If there is *one* civilian I trust, it's you," he said shaking his head. "Where's the truck now?"

"I suspect it's somewhere in the hospital parking lot."

"You want to tell me what it's doing in the hospital parking lot?"

"Not really."

Logan let out a deep sigh and headed for the door.

"Will."

"Yeah Ben?"

"Thank you. Don't forget to wipe the prints."

"Not gonna find a body in the truck-bed am I?" Will laughed, and walked out.

"You can come out now," Ben called to the bathroom door.

Kaitlyn poked her head out and looked down at him.

"Wow, you got a sheriff tucked away in your back pocket for emergencies. That could be handy," Kaitlyn said.

"No one's in anybody's pocket," Ben said, narrowing his eyes at her. "Will is a good friend."

"Yeah, well, no cop has ever agreed to cover things up to make *my* life any easier," she sneered.

"One just did Blythe. One just did."

* * *

"Roger Morgan, from the club, agreed to put in a good word at Stanford, should you decide you'd like a tour," Angela said to Cameron over their long dinner table.

"Not going to Stanford," he said, while still reading.

"Cameron, do me the honor of joining me for dinner, won't you?"

He sighed, folded his book, and then shoved it toward the center of the table.

"How is your dinner?" she asked. "I know roast beef and new potatoes are your favorite."

"It's delicious. You must have slaved all day in the kitchen preparing it."

"You know very well that Marta prepared dinner."

"Yes Mother, that was clearly a joke."

"So, if not Stanford, *where* then?"

"I haven't decided."

"What were you studying so diligently at the dinner table?" she asked smiling.

"You wouldn't like it, it's a history book."

"I've always enjoyed history. Share."

"This book is on *biblical* history," he said, slicing into his roast beef.

"Well, it's okay to be well rounded," she conceded.

"Really? You don't find the Bible to be controversial and pointless?"

"Cameron, you act as though I'm some kind of heathen. Of course I see the validity of biblical history. More than half the world believes in *something*. It would be close-minded to pretend there's nothing to it at all."

"Did you and Dad know that there are over three hundred-fifty prophecies in the old testament of a coming Messiah, which were all fulfilled by Jesus in his short lifetime?"

"I think personal religion is best left in private. The way to discuss it openly is to keep it on a general level."

"Bill and Olivia would sincerely disagree with that," he said out of the corner of his mouth.

"Perhaps the war, carnage, and civil unrest religion causes in the world has escaped them."

"Mom, has it occurred to you that some things just may be worth fighting for? Worth dying for?"

"Now religion is worth *dying* for? Do you hear yourself?"

"I know what you're thinking, but you're wrong. Not everyone who believes in God is ignorant."

"I didn't say they're ignorant. I just don't want those people filling your head with a bunch of nonsense. What's next? Going door to door with Bibles? Handing out flowers at the airport?"

"Bill and Olivia aren't part of a cult. They do more to care for people in one day, then all of your spoiled, self-serving friends do in a year."

"Cameron, that is highly unlikely. Do you have any idea how much money my *spoiled, self-serving* friends raised in benefits alone this past year?"

"Are you talking about the snooty parties you all throw, disguised as charity events, in a clever attempt to feel good about hobnobbing with the other elitist prigs? Because I feel like we've already covered this topic, Mom."

"Those benefits have helped more people than I can number. Why would you say such a thing?"

"Well, let me answer you this way. How many of the people you've helped do you know by name?"

"Charity work doesn't count unless you've slept in a gutter along side someone?"

"Here we go again," he sighed. "I'm saying, at the heart of these charitable functions, is a selfish motive. Sure, you feed people, you clothe them, you give away some money, which none of you would miss, and then write it off. Bravo."

"Are you suggesting that I stop making charitable contributions and spend all of our money on myself?"

"At least, *that* would be genuine," he said shaking his head. "Your money does help people, but giving from a distance, out of a surplus, is not the same thing as caring for them, and I wish for your sake you would stop confusing the two."

"Can we please change the subject and enjoy our dinner?"

"No need. I've lost my appetite," Cameron said, retrieving his book. "I'll be in my room."

11

Perchance to Care

KAITLYN HADN'T SEEN HER social worker in quite a while. When Lynn Bradley showed up at the children's home, Kaitlyn assumed that Ben told the cops about her breaking into that guy's house.

"Did she ever tell you where she was for those two days?" Lynn asked Molly, swiping some candy from the dish on her desk.

"Nope. Just showed up back here in a cab like she'd been on holiday without telling anyone where she'd gone."

"That kid's always been a little bit of a mystery to me," Lynn admitted.

"Is Kaitlyn being moved somewhere?" Molly asked.

"No one told you?"

Molly shook her head.

"Some guy wants guardianship."

"You're kidding," Molly said.

"That's why I'm here. This almost never happens at her age."

"It's Ben Gerard isn't it?" Molly asked.

"Yeah. How well do you know the guy?"

"Not all that well really. He had a run-in with her when she took off, the time before last. He started coming here shortly after."

"He's the one who's been making her read?" Lynn asked.

"Yep."

"Do you suppose she'd be better off with him?" Lynn asked.

"Better than living here until she ages out? Wouldn't they all be better off in homes?"

* * *

"You're going again aren't you?" Angela asked.

"The word is church Mom," Cameron said, eyeing her in the mirror, where he fastened his tie. "You're welcome to come unless you're afraid you'll be burned at the stake," he said, smirking.

Bill wouldn't have liked that. He re-thought his sarcastic invitation and kissed her cheek before leaving.

* * *

Kaitlyn looked around the house and put her bag down on the floor of the dining room. Caesar jumped onto the table beside her and she looked over at him.

"What do *you* want?" she asked.

"They're not really used to other people in the house—Probably excited to have some company," Ben said, leaning on his cane. His hip would need time to heal, though the doctor said he would likely need the cane for the rest of his life.

"Whatever," she said, ignoring Roofus, when he pushed his wet nose into her hand. "Where's my room?"

Ben led her through the dining room and Kaitlyn stopped to looked past the kitchen.

"What's in there?" she asked, looking at the room just between the kitchen and the back door.

"I suppose technically, that would be considered servant's quarters, though Rosie and I never had any servants."

"I want that room."

"No you don't. The washer dryer alone will drive you crazy. Also there's a tree outside of that window that rubs the house every time it storms . . . keep meaning to cut those branches."

"I don't care. I want that room."

"Blythe, it's half the size of the room I'm giving you."

"If you're worried about it being too close to the back door, don't. If I wanted to escape, sleeping down the hall from you wouldn't stop me."

"I suppose not," he nodded, realizing there was no point in trying to talk her out of the dinky little room. In truth, he wasn't at all fearful of her escape. He'd simply wanted to be a little generous with her.

* * *

Kaitlyn stared out the window of her tiny room. She didn't have much to unpack other than a few articles of clothing and her sketchbook. She knew it wasn't often that people like Ben came along, but every instinct she had told her not to trust it. How was it that someone like him existed in the same world where people could be so cruel? She wondered what her life would look like had her parents not died. Would the four of them have some family tradition on Sundays, like playing ball in a park somewhere, or riding bikes? Would she and Matty have woken up to countless pancake breakfasts? Would they have fought around the table, or gotten on like best friends? She pulled out her sketchbook and began to draw a house they may have all lived in. She had drawn it a hundred times, with only minor variations. She imagined it would be a two-story white house, not so big that they were rich, but in no way small. Two trees always donned the front yard. Sometimes they were barren with winter, sometimes full and green with spring blossoms. In a few of the sketches there was a tire-swing or a car in the driveway. Her room was upstairs right beside Matty's. She outlined the windows, as Ben called her to lunch, breaking into her thoughts.

"All settled in?" Ben asked, as she took a seat at the table.

"Not much to settle," she said, spooning some meat on to her plate.

Ben was surprised that she hadn't put up more of a fuss about his having guardianship, and though he didn't want to push her too far, too fast, he was hoping there was still enough room to build a better foundation in her.

"What *is* this anyway?" she asked, wrinkling her nose at the dish in front of her.

"Beef stroganoff. Rosie always made this on Sundays because she knew it was one of my favorites."

"Beef *what*?"

"You've never had beef stroganoff?"

"No, they usually serve caviar at the home on Sundays."

"I'm not as good a cook as my Rosie was, so don't expect much."

"Well don't over-sell it," she said, rolling her eyes.

As she brought the first fork-full to her mouth, Ben folded his hands in front of him. Kaitlyn held her fork above her plate and waited for him to finish.

"Lord, thank you for this food and this day. Thank you for all the many blessings you provide—the ones we see and the ones we don't. In Jesus name, amen."

Kaitlyn stared at him for a moment, contemplating his words and then stuffed her fork into her mouth.

Ben paused and raised his brows at her. She nodded and shrugged as though the food was fine and he nodded too.

* * *

"So are you ready for your last year?" Olivia asked Cameron, taking a sip of her lemonade.

"I am," he smiled.

"Which Ivy League school will have the pleasure of your company next year?" Bill asked.

"None of them," he said. "I've decided on a degree in philanthropic studies at a state school."

"That's great Cameron," said Olivia.

"John said you committed to twenty hours a week of volunteer work at the shelter. Will that interfere with your school work?" Bill asked.

"Nah. I wanted more hours but he said that was all he could do while I'm still in high school."

"How is your mom handling your educational decisions?" Bill asked.

"I haven't dropped that bomb yet."

"Don't you think she'll notice that you're not applying to or visiting any of the schools she and your dad had hoped for?"

"I'd like to think if my father were alive he'd understand . . . maybe even be encouraging."

"I'm sure he would," Olivia smiled.

"What did you think of the sermon?" Bill asked.

"I've worked out your formula, which has kind of a brilliant simplicity," Cameron said, in between bites of his hamburger.

"I'm all ears," Bill smiled.

"Don't give him a big head Cameron," Olivia chuckled.

"So, I notice you always begin by telling people that there is no hope of winning God's approval. I like how you include yourself in the mix though. I have been listening to sermons online and not many preachers tell people that they are, themselves, just as wicked as the people they're preaching to, like you do. In fact, most of them would insist that people turn away from their wickedness, which seems to be something that you want to make clear is here to stay. Though I'm not certain I agree with that."

"What about that gives you pause?" Bill asked.

"I'm just not sure it does a lot of good to think of ourselves as evil."

"That's because the world has trained you to think of evil only as it pertains to murderers and child molesters. In reality, God's standard is perfection, and none of us hit that mark."

"Let him finish," Olivia suggested.

"After you've convinced everyone that there is no hope, then you tell them the good news is that Jesus has died for them."

"Let me be clear," said Bill. "I only tell them there is no hope in themselves. It is a dangerous theology to think one can turn from sin and become sinless."

"But I thought the point of Christianity was that everyone was supposed to become good little boys and girls. Isn't faith in God supposed to cause a person to want to behave better?" Cameron asked. "If they aren't taught to be any different than the rest of the world, what's the difference between them and the rest of the world?"

"The desire to treat ones neighbor kindly comes from God. Of course we should treat others with kindness, but we fool ourselves if we think for one moment that there is no sin in us simply because we belong to God. With the thought that we climb some ladder, always getting better, always getting closer to God's will, is the danger of thinking more highly of ourselves than we ought. The point of Christianity is not good behavior. The point of Christianity is not to focus on what we, or our neighbors are doing, but to focus on what's been done for us. That kind of recognition would make someone *want* to behave, though we often fail, even in light of what God has done. Christianity is not a religion built on *good behavior*. It's the proclamation of a *gracious God*."

"I can certainly see the validity of dedicating ones life to helping other people. I'm just not certain I buy into the idea that there is a God who created all of this and all of us."

"What do you think is standing in the way of that belief?" Olivia asked.

"Simple. The world's a mess."

* * *

Ben got up from the table and began trying to clear the dishes. Kaitlyn watched him struggle a bit with his cane and pushed her chair out.

"I've got it, take a breather," she muttered, taking the dishes from him and turning on the water at the sink.

"I want to talk to you about your life," Ben said. "About your education, your future, and your brother Joshua."

"Matty," she corrected.

"I know that's where you were headed when you took off last time."

"Figure that out all by yourself did you?"

"They don't want you to have anything to do with him, but I think we can change that."

"Oh yeah? Enlighten me."

"They are afraid you'll be a bad influence on him. Maybe they're also afraid you'll steal his attention from them. I don't know."

"That's the stupidest thing I've ever heard."

"Well, it's not as though you haven't given people reason to think you're trouble Blythe. Look at this from their point of view for a moment."

"Why should I?" she snapped, drying her hands on a nearby towel. "Who's looked at this from *my* point of view? Where were they when *I* needed a home?"

"They were just a young couple looking to adopt a baby. They weren't trying to hurt anyone."

"If they didn't *want* us both then they should have *left* us both."

"Isn't there some part of you that's happy for your little brother?"

"Of course! I'm not a monster."

"The only way into his life is to stop behaving like a thug."

"Oh I see. If I get my act together you think these people will want me to come visit on holidays."

"I think you'll be less threatening."

"I'm not interested in being less threatening, I just want what they stole from me."

"They didn't steal your brother from you Blythe."

"Of course they did. He was all I had left after the accident. They took him. They changed his name. They never told him who he was."

"I know right now it seems hopeless, but it only *seems* that way. When you're young it feels like life will always be what it is right now. It won't. You have a whole lifetime to get to know him. Eventually he will find out he was adopted and he will want to know his biological family. It's human nature, and just a matter of time."

She stared at the wall in front of her.

"The dishes are done, I'll be in my room."

Kaitlyn hadn't slept all night since she was a baby. She usually stared at the ceiling or sketched by the moon's light when it was bright enough. Here at Ben's house she had a room to herself and the luxury of turning on a light, though she didn't feel like sketching. She got up and made her way down the hall. The house was dark and quiet. She heard Roofus grooming himself on the rug in the foyer and moved past him to the other rooms. She opened the door to the room Ben had wanted her to take and turned on the light. The room was much larger than the one she'd chosen, with a four-post bed and two dressers. There was a full-length mirror and a vanity table. She wondered if he had made the room pretty just for her or if it had always been this way. There was a light on in the walk-in closet. Inside she found, empty hangers, and empty shelves, but for one box. Blythe was written on the tag. She wondered why Ben hadn't mentioned it and took it back to her room.

Kaitlyn slipped into the new pajamas she'd found in the box and slid under the blanket. Perhaps she should have taken the other room. She rubbed the palms of her hands against the soft material and fell asleep.

* * *

Cameron pulled into the parking lot of Saint Raphael with a box of new toys. He had spent his entire month's allowance on them. He couldn't wait to see Jack's face when he opened the box. Jack met him at the door, as he had for the past few weeks since Cameron had been helping out at the shelter. He put the box down and gave Jack a high-five.

"What's that?" Jack asked, looking at the box.

"Why don't you open it and find out?"

Jack stuffed his little fingers between the box slit and pulled as hard as he could. Cameron watched his little face light up as he looked down at the shiny new toys.

"Are these for me?" Jack asked.

"For you and all of your friends too," Cameron said, rubbing the top of his head. "Check this out."

Cameron reached in, pulled out a remote control, and handed it to Jack. He reached into the box again and pulled out the car that mated the remote and placed it on the floor. He showed Jack how to make the car go and Jack took off after it.

"Cameron," John said, coming toward him with an outstretched hand. "You're showing up earlier and earlier."

"Wanted to get a jump on dinner."

Cameron had come to love helping out at the shelter, especially the dinners. He got to serve everyone and then sit and eat with John and Bill, when Bill could be there. Sometimes the three of them cleaned up together, and after the work was done, they would discuss what they'd need to keep going for another month. Cameron knew it was only a matter of time before he could get the proper funding to make the shelter bigger. He began to realize Bill was right about not alienating his mother. Now he'd set his sights on her charity work. If he could convince a few of those rich snobs to give to the shelter, he could make it a place of real refuge.

* * *

"Ben here?" Malachi asked.

"Out back," Kaitlyn said, letting him in.

"You must be Blythe, I'm Malachi."

"Good for you," she said, heading back to her room.

Malachi found Ben pulling up the weeds that had invaded Rosie's flowerbeds.

"Think maybe you ought to have your little convict doing that instead?"

"Hey Mal. What brings you out?"

"We've got planning to do."

Ben stood and Malachi handed him his cane, so they could head into the house.

"Still not gonna tell me how this happened huh?" Malachi asked.

"Forget it, it's not important."

"If I were the betting kind, I'd say it probably has something to do with your *houseguest.*"

Kaitlyn stood at her bedroom door wondering what Malachi was doing there.

"How many we got so far?" he asked.

"Not a one yet," Ben answered.

"Why don't you let me take over fishing on this one?" Malachi suggested.

"Are you trying to steal my job?"

"I can handle this," Malachi said, placing a glass of water in front of Ben.

"What if something were to happen?" Ben said, shaking his head.

"So, something more should happen to *you*? Listen, I'll talk to Logan about it. I can work with him as well as you can."

"I was thinking maybe we should skip this year," Ben said.

Just because you've got a criminal living here is no reason to skip the weekend."

Kaitlyn furrowed her brow, wondering what in the world that meant. What was it she was stopping Ben from doing?

"It was just a thought. I haven't decided what to do yet," Ben said. "Just think about it."

After Ben saw Malachi out, Kaitlyn made her way to the kitchen.

"What was that about?" she asked.

"Just business," Ben muttered.

Kaitlyn sat at the table and Caesar jumped up in her lap. She stroked his coat and pushed the water glass away from her.

"What is it you can't do because of me?"

"Nothing Blythe, forget it."

"Have it your way."

* * *

That night Kaitlyn found herself wandering the halls again. Ben had told her to make herself at home. He only asked that she stay out of the room at the end of the hall. It didn't take long before curiosity got the better of her and she went in, closing the door behind her as quietly as possible. She pushed a swipe mark through the dust on the dresser with her finger. Above the dresser was a framed picture of a teenaged boy. Ben was on one side of him and a woman on the other. Kaitlyn assumed she had been Ben's wife. The boy must have been their son. Posters of musicians scattered the walls and a couple of trophies stood on top of the outdated television set. She wondered where Ben's son was nowadays. Over the bed, the name Ray was spelled out in what looked like varsity jacket letters. She picked up the scrapbook from the desk and blew the dust from the cover before opening it. Newspaper clippings suggested Raymond Gerard had been some kind of local sports hero. His high school seemed to credit him for the all county win two years in a row. A few of the words were lost on her but she got the idea. She opened the closet door and had a look around. A trunk lay on the closet floor. She pulled open the lid, taking great care not to let it bump the wall. Beneath the football, baseball mitt, and a couple of sports magazines, was a pile of notebooks. She picked one up and flipped it open. It had dated entries. These were journals—Ben's son's journals. Kaitlyn tucked a couple of them under her arm and pulled the lid back over the trunk. She closed the closet door, and then shut the lamp on the bedside table and quietly made her way back to her room.

* * *

When Malachi saw Ben pull into Schrader's PC Repair he closed the laptop he'd been working on.

"Time for lunch?" Ben asked from the counter.

Malachi nodded and yelled into the back room that he was going to Annie's.

Ben ordered his usual club soda with a lemon wedge and before Malachi could order his drink, Rocky came out from behind the counter.

"I got this," she said to the younger waitress.

"Hey Rock, how's things?" Ben smiled.

"I wanted to thank you again for getting Cameron straightened out."

"Everything okay now?"

"Better than ok," Rocky beamed. "Though my sister Angela might tell a different story."

"Well, I'll come for breakfast soon. You'll have to tell me all about it," Ben said.

She realized then that Ben and Malachi must have had a limited time for their lunch meeting. She took their order and left them to their private discussion.

"What's up?" Malachi asked.

"I have an idea. I think it's a good one, but I need your help."

"I've been known to help you here and there."

"What would you think of putting on a weekend, if there was only one fish?"

Malachi eyed him as he drank his soda.

"Gee Ben, I don't know," he said, shaking his head.

"It's no less important work in smaller numbers right?" Ben asked.

"Of course not, but she isn't the most agreeable fish I've ever met."

"The whole itinerary will take some re-configuring," Ben added.

"You've already dropped all charges on her. What makes you think she would be in any way motivated to agree to the terms of the weekend?"

"Nothing."

Malachi took another sip of soda and smiled at Ben as his mind began to work out the details.

"One fish huh?" he mused.

"Minnow," Ben said, nodding.

* * *

Angela watched Cameron charm her friends. She was proud of him, although she thought his new religion was a waste of time. She wondered what those church people had done to captivate him.

"I think all the volunteer work Cameron's doing at the homeless shelter will look fantastic on his applications," said Marjorie Whitmore.

"I quite agree," her husband, Davis said, making his way over to them.

"I think my son is out to save the world," Angela said.

"Do I detect a note of sarcasm?" Davis chuckled.

"He's young," Marjorie said. "Give him time."

"I'm hoping he learns the difference between taking thousands off the street with a degree from Harvard, and shuttling four or five to a fast-food restaurant in a station wagon."

Davis and Marjorie couldn't help but giggle.

"Surely any boy of Warren Stowe's has the good sense to leave trash on the street where it belongs," Davis said.

Angela looked over at her son above the rim of her wine goblet.

"One can only hope Davis. One can only hope."

* * *

Ben watched Kaitlyn eat breakfast swaddled in the pajamas he'd bought for her. She sat on the kitchen chair, with her knees drawn up to her chest, the way a little girl would, as she ate her cereal. He smiled as another idea surfaced.

"Is there something on my chin?" she asked.

"No."

"What gives?" she said, shrugging.

He shook his head and went back to his crossword puzzle.

* * *

The next gift had to be special enough for Kaitlyn to know that Ben was intent on sharing with her a love that only came from God. Ben placed the box on the shelf in the closet and left the light on. He left the door to the room open, hoping she would see the light from the closet. He excused himself to bed, leaving her on the couch watching television. When at last she turned off all the lights to go to bed, she saw the faint glow coming from the hallway. When Kaitlyn went into the closet, she saw the box. She couldn't help but smile to herself. She switched off the closet light and carried the gift back to her room. The box was filled with charcoal pencils for sketching and a sketchpad. She pulled them out and beneath them she found paints and canvas. On the bottom of the box was a note.

I pray these things offer you an outlet to process the pain this life has caused. No matter where you go, or who you become, know that you are loved, Kaitlyn Blythe.

She put all the contents back in the box. She placed the box on her bedside table and then drifted to sleep with the note in her hands.

* * *

Cameron scooped some mashed potatoes on to Henry's tray. He'd only been coming around for the past week or two.

"Can I have just one more scoop?" Henry asked, his glassy blue eyes begging. Cameron knew he had been drinking and could use more food. His body looked emaciated, the deep lines in his face telling a story his mouth could never make up.

"If I give you more, there may not be enough for everyone," Cameron said, with a pit in his stomach.

Henry nodded and Cameron handed him a roll. This was the only part of being here that Cameron hated. This was the part that made him hate his mother for not allowing him to break into his bank account. Bill saw the look on his face and broke in.

"Cameron, can you go and prepare the coleslaw for tomorrow's lunch?"

"But there are so many people who haven't eaten yet," Cameron said, looking at the people in line.

"I've got this," Bill said, taking the ladle from his hand.

Cameron reluctantly handed over his utensil and pushed his way through the kitchen doors.

* * *

Bill pulled the can of chewing tobacco from his pocket and opened it to take a pinch. The smell of cherry tobacco wafted by in the breeze.

"How does Olivia feel about that?" Cameron asked, pointing to the little tin in his hands.

"About like you'd suspect I suppose."

"Can I try some?" Cameron asked.

"You're funny."

"Perhaps it's just as bad an idea for you then," Cameron smirked.

"Touché," said Bill, returning the can to his pocket.

Cameron grabbed the wastebasket and held it in front of his friend.

Bill sighed and took the tin from his pocket, then tossed it into the trash.

"It's difficult not to take every face and every problem home with me when I leave here," Bill said.

"I know what you mean," Cameron muttered.

"But I had to learn not to do that, and so do you."

Cameron looked at him as though Bill was disappointed. Bill didn't want the kid getting empathy fatigue right out of the starting gate.

"I see them when I'm falling asleep at night," Cameron admitted. "Did that happen to you?"

"Yeah. Doing this kind of work effectively takes some practice."

"What do you mean?" Cameron asked.

"You can get buried under the weight of putting in too many hours, or adopting the problems of other people, and when that happens your no good to them or to yourself. John and I would like to see you pull back a little."

"You two discussed this already?" he asked. "You're cutting my hours?"

"No Cameron. You're a grown man. We were hoping you would make the decision yourself."

"What decision is that?"

117

"The decision to have a life outside of this place. You're a senior in high school. Enjoy that. Every Friday night you're here serving dinner, and that's great, but what about dating? What about football games?"

"I'm not into sports and I'm pretty certain that the girls I am interested in haven't gotten the memo that I live on this planet."

"It only seems that way now," Bill chuckled. "Once a young woman gets a look at that heart of yours that'll change, you'll see."

"You're telling me to turn into the skid?"

"Exactly."

* * *

Ben could hardly believe his eyes when he opened the envelope from Kaitlyn's school. He went to Rosie's greeting card box and picked out an appropriate card to leave in Kaitlyn's closet. That night when she turned down the lights before bed she found his card.

> Ms. Blythe,
> Please accept my invitation to dinner in celebration of your exceptional interim report. In the box, please find a new dress, which you reserve the right to wear or not wear to dinner. I'm very proud of you,
> Ben

She flipped the box open and pulled the dress against her. It was a lovely blue, which would fall just below her knees. She hadn't worn a dress since she was five. She folded it neatly and placed it back in the box. She took the note and placed it in her night table drawer on top of Ben's other notes. From his room he heard Kaitlyn close her bedroom door to go to sleep and he smiled to himself.

12

Weight of the World

"CAMERON, CAN I SPEAK to you for a moment?" his mother asked, poking her head into his room.

"*May* you? Yes you may. *Can* you? That's entirely up to you Mom," he said, not taking his eyes from his computer.

"Cameron. Downstairs. Now."

"I was actually in the middle of an important project," he said, sauntering down the stairs with his hands stuffed in his pockets.

"Sit down," she said, ignoring him. "I've accepted this new you. I've looked the other way while you've made questionable decisions. I've even shrugged off your disrespect toward me, chalking it up to an age-appropriate rebellion, but now I have to put my foot down."

"Don't tell me . . . my socks don't match my trousers."

"Did you call Roger Morgan and ask him to donate his money to that . . . that *shelter*?"

"Relax Mom, shelter isn't a dirty word."

"This isn't a joke Cameron. It's getting embarrassing now."

"I'm an embarrassment? Why? Because I care about what happens to my friends?"

"Your *friends*? Do you hear yourself?"

"They may be trash to be left on the street to you, but to me, they're people."

"What are you talking about?" she asked, folding her arms.

"Don't bother feigning ignorance. I heard your conversation with your cronies at the benefit."

"I'm giving you a list of acceptable universities to which you may apply. I want your applications in by the end of the week."

"What makes you think you have anything to say about where I attend school?"

"As long as you're living in *my* house, I have *everything* to say about it."

"Then maybe my time would be better spent finding a new place to live."

* * *

Kaitlyn pulled her new dress from the box and hung it in the closet of her little room. She looked down at her sneakers. It hadn't occurred to Ben to buy her shoes. She wouldn't have felt like herself in the dress anyway, she reasoned, brushing her hand against it. She stopped in the doorway wondering if that would be such a bad thing.

* * *

Malachi, Rick, Frankie, and Lucius sat at the round table in the meeting room at Camp Trinity for the first time since the previous Consuming Fire weekend.

"Thank you all for coming," Ben said.

"Is this it?" Frankie asked. "There were a lot more guys working on my weekend."

"This is just the kitchen crew right?" Rick asked.

"This weekend will be a little different than any of the others we've done."

"How many have we got so far?" Rick asked, pulling a piece of gum from his pocket.

"That's what I'd like to talk about."

* * *

"Cameron, what's up?" Bill said, answering his phone.

"I might need to crash out at your place for a while, if that's okay."

"Has something happened?"

"My mother is being ridiculous about school and I told her I'd find somewhere else to be if it was going to keep coming up."

"Define *ridiculous*."

"She wants to literally give me a list of schools to which I am allowed to apply."

"Have you looked at the list?" Bill asked.

"I don't have to. I know full-well which schools will be on it."

"Why do you assume that you can't help people while taking advantage of the things your parents have to offer?"

"It just seems like a waste of money—money better spent elsewhere."

"Cameron, has it not occurred to you that your father worked long and hard to make sure you got a first rate education?"

"Yeah."

"Well then has it occurred to you that God, in his infinite wisdom, has seen to it that someone in your financial position has a heart for the weak and the helpless?"

"You're saying God won't be happy unless I'm rowing on a crew-team somewhere?"

"I'm saying, it would be silly of you to not take advantage of the opportunities you have. What you *do*, not where you come from, will determine who you are."

"What if it turns me into someone I don't like?"

"It's very likely that you'll have those days anyway. We all do."

* * *

In a matter of months Kaitlyn had gone from an elementary to a high school reading level. Ben worked with her every day after school without realizing he was teaching her to read Ray's journals. Ray was an anomaly. He was a good student, active in sports, and had the heart of a poet. His journal entries sometimes moved Kaitlyn to tears. He seemed to be a friend to everyone he met. She blew through the first two journals and went back for more, careful to look at the dates so that she could read them chronologically.

* * *

"I'll make you a deal," Cameron said to his mother. "I'll apply to your schools, if you let me have some of my trust fund money."

"Out of the question. That money is designated to pay off your education."

"I can get some scholarships, and I can apply for grants, and a work-study program. I give you my word that my education won't bury me in debt."

"Your father didn't want you to have to do those things. He wanted you to be able to start fresh. Cameron, he started saving for your college tuition before you were even born. He would be angry with me for even considering letting you touch it for anything else."

"Wherever he is now, he realizes that helping other people is a worthy cause."

"Wherever he *is*? He's dead. You know he didn't believe in life after death. What he did believe was that you can't help anyone until you've helped yourself."

"Mom listen to me, I know I've been hard on you. At times I've been rude, sarcastic, and even downright mean."

Angela's eyes filled at the sincerity of his tone.

"Answer one question. If Dad were here now, if he could see me—who I am, what I want to do . . . would he be *disappointed*? Or would he be *proud*?"

A tear fell from her face as she looked at him. She thought about what Warren would say if he were there.

"Proud," she whispered.

Cameron smiled and reached for her hand.

"So then . . . do we have a deal?"

* * *

Kaitlyn's tailor-made Consuming Fire weekend was in the final planning stages. Ben was always impressed by the men's willingness to come together and be a team for the sake of another person. Rick and Frankie had become a two-man kitchen and dining crew, Oscar and Gene told Ben they would serve anywhere they were needed. Ben and Bill were going to do the spiritual leading, with Lucius praying non-stop in the back ground, while Malachi focused on all things travel-related. Now Ben just had to get her there.

* * *

In a strange way, Kaitlyn began to feel as though Ray was her closest friend. His journals were overflowing with love for his parents. Rosie seemed to have been the type of mother who was as kind and affectionate as she was supportive and encouraging. It seemed that even in adolescence, Ray had great respect for his father too. Ben's gift of wisdom seemed to have a profound effect on his son and she wondered if he knew that. She assumed the three of them had spent many happy years in this house. Now, only one of them was left. Ray had to have been dead. The kind of relationship he'd had with his father simply would not have allowed for a long estrangement.

* * *

Cameron said goodnight to John and pulled the convertible into the alley behind the shelter. Jack's mother Nora took him by the hand and Cameron waved for them to get into the car. He knew better than to tell John or Bill about his plans to help them through their spell. He knew Bill would try to talk him out of it. With the two of them safely in the back of the car, he headed for home. For the first time in his life Cameron said a prayer. As he looked into the rear-view mirror and saw Nora pull Jack into her arms, he prayed that his mother would not be home when he got there.

"Where are we going?" Jack asked.

"It's a surprise," Cameron smiled. "We're going to play a game when we get there."

"What kind of game?"

"It's kind of like hide and seek. You have to be very good at it."

"How do you play?" Jack asked.

"You have to be very quiet and listen to your mother," he said.

Nora pulled him in closer and kissed the top of his head.

"Thank you," she said to Cameron when she caught his eyes in the mirror.

Cameron pulled into his long driveway and headed for the little guest-house in back.

"Are we going to live here?" Jack asked.

"Just for now," Cameron said, looking around. His mother's car was still gone. He opened the back door and put a finger to his lips. "Okay buddy, let's start our game now. Be very quiet and follow me."

The two of them followed him into the guesthouse. He pulled the heavy curtains closed and turned on a small lamp.

"You can put your bags in whichever room you'd like," Cameron told them. "I put a few things in the pantry and the refrigerator. I'll come by in the morning."

Nora looked around in disbelief. It seemed a bit like a dollhouse. Every wall was decorated with colors and patterns. The air was thick with the smell of vanilla and fresh linens. The rug was soft and thick beneath their feet. Jack ran to the baby grand, which was tucked in the dining room and his mother pulled him back.

"Remember, we need to stay quiet," she said. "Let's get cleaned up."

She stayed away from the master bed and bath, feeling as though that would be intrusive somehow. Instead she and Jack made their way down the hall to a guest-room. Jack ran to the built in bench window and hopped up on it. Nora wondered how this beautiful house could be simply a place for guests.

"I like it here," Jack said swinging his legs.

"Me too," she said smiling at him.

* * *

Kaitlyn had become somewhat accustomed to the notes and gifts Ben had been leaving her. She wasn't surprised when she saw the glow of the closet light again and went to fetch his latest present. This time it was just an envelope. She brought it back to her room and opened it.

> Ms. Blythe,
>   It is my every hope that you will accept this invitation to a special weekend getaway. If you do, there will be instructions and provisions to follow,
>   Ben

She was puzzled by the invitation. Why hadn't he simply told her they were going away somewhere? What kind of instructions and provisions would she need for a weekend trip? She shut her lamp and fell asleep.

* * *

Cameron hurried through the shelter, making certain he had checked off everything on his chore list before heading out.

"I'm glad to see you cutting back on your hours a bit," John said to him.

"Yeah, I have a lot going on. Please let me know if there's anything more you need from me," Cameron said, brushing the counter with a wet rag and tossing it in the sink.

"Are you signed up to serve dinner tomorrow night?" John asked.

"Yes. I may be a little late. I mean I can't come right after school like I usually do, but I'll be here before dinner."

"That's fine. You don't have to come so early anyway."

"I don't mind," Cameron said, picking up a box from the floor.

"Cameron?"

"I know, girls, football, extracurricular activities. I've got it."

"Keys?" John smiled, holding out Cameron's car keys.

"Oh right—wouldn't get too far without those."

"Are you all right?" John asked.

"Yeah. Just running late," he said, heading for the door.

Bill walked in as he was leaving.

"Where are you off to in such a hurry?"

"I'm late meeting a friend," Cameron said, walking backward toward the parking lot.

"How's the car running?" Bill yelled.

"It's great. Sorry—got to go."

Bill bent down to pick up some trash outside the back door and noticed Cameron driving off with Henry in the passenger seat.

"What are you doing?" Bill murmured to himself.

* * *

When Cameron arrived at home he saw his mother's car in the driveway.

"Duck down," he said to Henry as he headed toward the guesthouse.

Angela walked out on to the front porch. She had been waiting to talk to him. When she noticed he drove back to the guesthouse, she followed.

"What are you doing parked way back here?"

Cameron motioned to Henry that he should stay down and tried to get out of the car quickly to keep her from noticing him crouched on the floorboard.

"I was just giving you room. Doesn't your bridge-club meet tonight?"

"Yes, but there's plenty of room for you in the driveway. I've been doing some thinking. I suppose if you'd like to work while you're in school that would be all right. There's nothing wrong with working hard. I guess with some scholar—"

"Mom, do we have to talk about this right now?"

"Cameron, what on earth is the matter with you? I am trying to offer an olive branch here."

He looked over and saw Nora looking out the window.

"You're right. Let's go and talk about this," he said, as he put an arm around his mother's waist and led her back to the main house.

* * *

Kaitlyn was in bed reading another of Ray's journals when she heard Ben call her to dinner. Ray had become a mentor to this kid Jason, who seemed to Kaitlyn, a hopeless case. Ray reminded her a great deal of Ben. He wrote about the potential he saw for his friend Jason to do well in school and maybe try out for some of the teams. Ray had also begun to write about a girl named Jasmine quite often. She shut the book and slid it beneath her pillow.

"Mind setting the table?" Ben asked.

She took two plates down from the cabinet and then stared at them on the table.

"You still with me Blythe?" Ben joked.

"Huh?"

"Were you sketching?" he asked, stirring the pot on the stove.

"No."

She stared at him, wondering what on earth had happened to Ray.

"Blythe . . . you okay?"

"Yeah. I was studying—sort of."

"Well, let's eat—sort of," Ben said smiling.

"How long did you and your wife live here?" she asked.

"Oh, I suppose twenty-five years or so, until she passed."

"Just the two of you?" she asked, pushing a forkful of food into her mouth.

He put his fork down and cleared his throat.

"Have you given any thought to my invitation?" he asked.

"Where exactly am I being invited to?"

"You'll just have to trust me Blythe."

"Do I have to decide right now?"

"Not at this moment, but a lot of planning needs to be done, so as soon as you know, I'd like to know."

She wondered if perhaps he was going to take her to see Matty.

* * *

Bill counted and re-counted the bags of rice in the pantry. He had noticed shortages on his inventory list of a few other items as well. He pulled on the padlock and shook his head.

"Everything okay Bill?" John asked, shutting the kitchen light.

"Yeah. Did Cameron leave yet?"

"I'm right here," Cameron said, heading for the back door.

"Can you stick around?" Bill asked.

"Can't tonight. I'm still under mom's deadline to fill out applications."

"Some other time then," Bill said, eyeing the kid.

"Sure thing. Night."

Bill walked out the back door and leaned against the wall. He watched Cameron make a left instead of a right and then stop in the alley and pick someone up.

* * *

Ray had taken Jason under his wing, and Kaitlyn had the distinct feeling that it was going to be a mistake. She was now into his third year of high school and he had started dating Jasmine. Most of his entry's about her seemed far away, whimsical even. Kaitlyn could tell he loved her, before he'd even realized it himself. He'd spent half a page describing her smile. Kaitlyn couldn't imagine anyone feeling that way about her. Most of her life's focus had been on her mere survival. For the first time she was sleeping through the night. She felt free to concentrate on her schoolwork, and she was excelling quickly. Ben had even talked to her about attending college. She slid Ray's journal into her bedside table drawer and shut the light. Ray had been dating Jasmine without ever writing about being intimate with her. She turned it over and over in her mind and she couldn't make sense of any of it. What kind of a guy would rather talk about marrying a girl than seducing her? The kids Kaitlyn knew from school didn't think twice about that sort of thing. Sex was as common a bodily function for those kids as sneezing. Ray had talked about things like integrity, goals, real friendship, and commitment. He wrote often about the things his parents had taught him to treasure. Now he was teaching those things to her.

* * *

John, Bill, and Cameron sat together on the back porch of the shelter watching the sunset for the first time in quite a while.

"You know what's odd?" Bill asked.

"What's that?" John said.

"The people who've spelled in the past couple of weeks don't seem to have made their way back here at meal time like they usually do."

Cameron shot Bill a look.

"I've noticed that," John agreed.

Bill used one of his fingernails to clean the others and shook his head.

"Any ideas about that Cam?" he murmured.

Cameron cleared his throat and squinted out toward the sunset, shaking his head.

"Maybe they've found some new shelter with a better cook than you," he joked.

"Hmmm. Maybe."

Bill looked right through the kid.

"Where were you and Henry off to that night you tore out of here?" he asked.

"What?" Cameron said, chuckling.

"I saw you pick up Henry and leave here together one night. What was that about?"

"Oh right," Cameron said. "He needed a ride uptown."

John's cell phone rang and he excused himself to speak privately.

"We have a very tight budget here Cam," Bill said.

"I know that."

"The pantry inventory has been off for the past couple of weeks. Can you tell me why?"

"How would *I* know?"

"I believe you do."

"Are you accusing me of sneaking in here for midnight snacks?" Cameron said, laughing. "Because I can certainly afford my own rice and beans Bill."

"How did you know rice and beans are what's missing?"

Cameron swallowed hard and shrugged his shoulders.

"You can't do this Cameron. It's a bad idea for so many reasons."

"You sound like my mother."

"This is not the way to help these people."

"Yeah, food and shelter is really going to spoil them rotten."

"Where are you keeping them?"

Cameron shook his head.

"Not your mother's house? What if she finds them there and calls the police?"

"She won't. They're out in the guesthouse."

"She will. It's only a matter of time. I'm afraid this might do more harm than good," Bill insisted.

"I didn't know what else to do!" Cameron yelled. "They were going to end up on the street."

"Rely on a system that works, that's what we do."

"When a little boy is frightened and sleeping in doorways at night and I have a perfectly good house not being used, I would say the damn system has broken down Bill!"

"Cameron listen—"

"I'll replace the rice and beans," he said, bounding down the steps toward the convertible.

"What was *that* about?" John asked, coming back outside.

"Do you remember being young enough to believe you could save the world?" Bill said, shaking his head.

* * *

Ben was kneeling at his bedside when he heard footsteps. He saw a piece of paper sail beneath the crack of the door and leaned over to pick it up.

> I accept,
>   Blythe

He smiled to himself and finished his prayers, some of which were answered by those three words.

* * *

Angela eyed Marta carefully before excusing her for the evening. She had worked for the Stowe family for twenty years. Surely Angela couldn't have misread her all this time.

"Marta, is anything going on in your life that you would like to talk about?"

"No Ma'am," Marta answered, wrapping her sweater around her shoulders and retrieving her pocketbook.

"If there is, I hope you know you can always come to me."

"Of course Mrs. Stowe."

"Do you feel that I pay you adequately?"

"Yes," Marta said, furrowing her brow.

"And you have *nothing* to say to me?"

"Thank you?" Marta said.

"I'll see you in the morning," Angela sighed.

She was almost certain money had been taken from her wallet. It was the third time that week. She had never known Marta to steal. She hoped she was mistaken about the amount of cash she'd had on hand, or that if Marta had indeed taken it, it solved whatever issue she was having.

* * *

Shuffling people between the shelter and the guesthouse had become quite a job for Cameron. He didn't know how much longer he could keep this up without his schoolwork or volunteer job at the shelter suffering. He dropped Henry in the alley behind the shelter and pulled around to the parking lot. Bill tossed him his apron as he walked into the kitchen and Cameron took his place behind the counter, grabbing a ladle.

"Hey Henry, haven't seen you in a while," Bill said, spooning some chipped beef on to his tray.

Henry looked over at Cameron and he handed him a roll and a scoop of potatoes.

"Amazing how you two arrived here at *exactly* the same time, on the day Henry's spell is up," Bill smirked.

"Are we going to play games now?" Cameron asked, while serving the next person in line. "You know where he's been. I never lied to you about it, and I'm not going to apologize for it either. I replaced all the food I took to feed my people."

"*Your* people?" Bill muttered. "That's disturbing."

"Yeah well, at least I'm doing something about it."

"Meaning I'm not?" Bill said. He stopped what he was doing and looked at the kid.

"Look, I'm not saying that. I just mean trying to go through all the red tape is frustrating. Come winter, these people need warm beds."

"What you're doing is a temporary fix at best."

"Well, I'm open to ideas Bill."

* * *

"Maybe you should just let him help them," Olivia said, rubbing Bill's shoulders.

"How can you say that? This has disaster written all over it."

"He's just trying to do whatever he can for them. Is that really so awful?"

"Of course not. I am secretly hoping he *doesn't* get caught—I'm cheering for the kid Liv, but it's the wrong way to go about this."

She nodded and took a deep breath.

"Regardless, I'm proud of him Bill."

"Me too. That heart came out of nowhere," Bill said, shaking his head.

* * *

Kaitlyn put her schoolbooks away and reached for Ray's journal. She had read as far as his being a senior in high school. Jasmine had become the love of his life. His friend Jason was more troubled than ever. He had begun using drugs and Ray wouldn't dare ask his parents for help. Ray wrote that Ben firmly believed that once a person became an addict it would take a miracle to bring them back from their addiction. It seemed to be the only thing he and Ben disagreed about. It seemed Jason's family was going to have to move. His father had run off and Jason's mother couldn't afford to keep up with their house payments. From what she'd read, Ben and Rosie were pretty comfortable financially, and she wondered if Jason's addiction was the only reason he hadn't asked them to help his friend. Ray tried to help him whenever he could. He had been buying the kid's lunch since their sophomore year.

"The acorn sure doesn't fall far from the tree," she whispered into the quiet of her room. She fell back against her pillow wondering if she should simply come right out and ask about Ray.

13

Little Minnow

KAITLYN SLIPPED ON HER sneakers when she heard the car pull up.

"You all set?" Malachi asked.

"I guess so."

"These your bags?"

She nodded and when she bent down to pick one up, he stopped her.

"Are you going to tell me where you're taking me?" she asked when Malachi slid into the driver's seat.

"Farrow Island."

"Where's Ben?"

Malachi adjusted the rear-view mirror and placed his fishing hook around it.

"He's already out there. He said to give you this," he said, handing her a card.

> Kaitlyn,
>
> I'm so happy that you've agreed to go away on this very special weekend. I pray that this is a new beginning for you. I want to reassure you that even though we all go through difficult things, the Lord our God, is always with us. See you soon,
>
> Ben

* * *

Cameron read his acceptance letter from Stanford realizing he was among an elite few who would ever receive such an invitation. He placed it on his desk and looked out the bedroom window toward the guesthouse.

* * *

Rick poked his head out of the kitchen when he heard the car pull up.

"Minnow on deck," he called out, and Ben went out to greet her.

"Welcome to Camp Trinity," Ben said smiling.

"So this is where you take all your convicts," she said, looking around.

"I see Malachi took the liberty of explaining some things on the ride over."

Malachi winked at her and grabbed her bags.

"I'll show you to your room, and you can get washed up for dinner," Ben told her.

* * *

Cameron came down the stairs and saw Marta walking out the front door.

"If you're going to the store, can you please add a few things to the grocery list?" he asked.

"I'm not going to the store," she said, and closed the door behind her.

"What was *that* about?" he asked, turning to his mother.

"Marta has been stealing. She's been let go," she said, picking up the phone.

"What?"

"Hold on Cameron, I have to call the temp agency to see if I can get someone to cover the week while I look for new help."

He looked out the front doors and saw Marta making her way toward the bus stop.

"Mom, you can't fire her!" he pleaded.

"Cameron hold on—hello, this is Mrs. Stowe. I'm going to need a temp."

Cameron hurried out the front door and caught up with Marta.

"Stop, wait! What's going on?"

"Your mother has some crazy idea in her head that I've been stealing. I've never stolen anything in my life."

"There must be some mistake."

"That's what I tried to tell her."

"Come back to the house, we'll get this all straightened out," he called, as she walked away.

Trying to fund his makeshift shelter in the back yard had become anything but easy. His mother hadn't given him nearly the amount of money he was hoping for from his school account. He watched Marta continue to shuffle down the sidewalk toward the bus stop and ran back into the house.

"You can't fire Marta."

"Don't be ridiculous. I won't employ a thief. By day's end she won't be able to get a job anywhere in the county," Angela muttered, picking up the phone again.

* * *

Kaitlyn sat in the midst of the dining room as the team hurried around preparing dinner. Malachi took a seat across from her and placed a glass of lemonade in front of each of them. Ben sat and folded his hands.

"What am I doing here?" Kaitlyn asked.

"Just let the weekend unfold," Ben proposed. "It's different for everyone, but basically, the goal is to leave here without some of the wrong ideas you've been carrying around."

"Well, what's for dinner?" she asked, as Rick made his way over to the table.

"Fresh Ahi, rolled in sesame, finished in my secret sauce," Rick smiled.

He put the platter on the table and Kaitlyn wrinkled her nose at it.

"That fish is practically raw," she sneered.

"You might find that you like it," Ben said.

"You first," she said to Malachi.

He stabbed a tender slice with his fork, brushed it against the wasabi paste, and stuffed it into his mouth. He closed his eyes and smiled.

"No one—and I mean, *no one* makes Ahi like Rick," he said, reaching for his lemonade.

"I'm warning you all right now, if this tastes like smelly old fish I'm going to spit it out."

Rick rolled his eyes and stabbed at a slice with a fork, then brushed it against the wasabi and brought it to her mouth.

"Open," he said, jiggling the tuna filled fork in front of her as though she was five.

She closed her eyes and opened her mouth, bracing herself as it landed on her tongue.

"That's *fish*?" she asked, with her eyes wide. "Why does it taste like meat?"

Rick smiled and set the fork down on the napkin in front of her.

"Now that we have your approval," Ben said, "let's begin our weekend."

He bowed his head and the men all followed suit.

"Father, we want to thank you for the opportunity to spend time thinking about you and your word. We especially thank you for this food and the willingness of the team to come out and serve. We ask for special blessings on Kaitlyn, and pray that she begins to see you more clearly."

He opened his eyes then and nodded at the men, before officially beginning the weekend.

"Therefore let us be grateful for receiving a kingdom that cannot be shaken, and thus let us offer to God acceptable worship, with reverence and awe, for our God is a consuming fire."

After Ben quoted the verse the men all applauded and Kaitlyn wondered why.

"Well, this is a first," Gene said.

Kaitlyn looked at him and shook her head.

"Usually the fish are all boy-types," Rick explained.

"Never had a girl take your bike?" Kaitlyn asked, pulling more Ahi on to her plate.

"You're the first," Ben said.

"I'm pretty sure you're also the first fish he's ever adopted," Oscar said chuckling.

"Do you all wear those hooks around your necks to remind you that you're nothing but fish?" she asked.

Rick sat back smiling and ran his fingers against the line around his neck.

"Oh, but we aren't," he said to her.

"The hooks remind us that we're fishers of men," said Malachi.

"Fishers of *men*? What is that, some kind of club?"

"Something like that," he answered.

"Yeah, Frankie is our newest club member," Rick laughed, scruffing his head.

"Don't suppose there's any food left," Lucius said, walking in.

Kaitlyn almost gasped at the size of him.

"Sorry I'm late," he said, pulling up a chair.

"The food's been pre-blessed," Frankie said.

"You must be Kaitlyn. I'm Lucius."

She watched her hand get swallowed up inside of his when he shook it. He could have crushed her easily if he'd wanted to. His arms had to have been as wide as her legs, maybe wider.

"For tonight," Ben continued, "I'd like you to think about Hebrews 12:28–29. That was the verse I quoted just before we ate. Underline it in the Bible that's been left in your room. I also want you to think about your future. Give some thought to what you'd like to do, who you'd like to be, and we'll discuss it in the morning."

* * *

"I can't help out at the shelter tonight," Cameron said to Bill. "My mother is having company and I have to keep an eye on things around here."

"You *know* you have to stop what you're doing, right?"

"Are we going to rehash this every time we talk now Bill?"

"In a few years you'll be in a position to do a lot of people a lot of good, but right now—"

"Do you think they can wait a few years to eat, or to sleep in warm beds? They need me *now*."

"Is this about *them* or your *need* to be needed?" Bill asked. "The thing about Robin Hood is that when you get past the romance of it all, he's just a thief—plain and simple."

"I told you, I already replaced the food in the pantry."

"What about Marta? You effectively took her job and her reputation. Doesn't it matter what happens to *her*? Or are we now subscribing to some sort of utilitarianism to support the cause?"

"I'll find a way to help her," Cameron sighed. "I've got to go."

Bill hung up the phone and looked at Olivia.

"How is he?" she asked.

"I almost miss the old Cameron. At least when we first met he *knew* he was acting like an idiot."

* * *

Kaitlyn underlined the passage in Hebrews as Ben had instructed. Although these men had clearly put a lot of thought into the weekend, she couldn't help but feel disappointed that she wasn't going to Atlanta to see her brother. She closed the Bible and opened Ray's journal. Jason wanted to start selling drugs in order to make some fast money and help his mom hold on to her house. Ray tried to discourage it, but Jason seemed to have his own ideas. Though Kaitlyn had developed a genuine admiration for Ray, she found herself relating to Jason on some level. After all, what did Ray know about having it rough? He had a loving home, complete with two parents who'd done nothing but encourage him. She couldn't fault him for that. She couldn't help but resent him for it a little too. As she closed the journal it occurred to her that Ben had been trying to give her the same loving home, the same encouragement.

* * *

Cameron opened the door to the guesthouse carrying a box filled with hot sandwiches for dinner and heard someone playing the piano. He placed the box on the dining table, where Nate and Dana sat listening to the music.

"Quinton right?" Cameron said to the pianist.

He nodded and tossed back his long, curly hair, as he reached into the box for a sandwich.

"Where'd you learn to play like that?"

"My mom's been teaching since before I was born," he said, stuffing his mouth.

"Nate, were you able to get the toilet to stop running?" Cameron asked.

Nate nodded and waved his children over for dinner.

"I need a headcount," Cameron said to Michelle, as he made his way into the living room.

"Twenty-two as of this morning," she said, getting up from the couch.

Cameron took a water bottle from the refrigerator and gulped down half of it as his eyes darted from window to window. As he was wondering how easily someone could see inside the house at night he noticed a giant red stain on the living room carpet.

"One of the kids spilled a glass of fruit punch," Michelle said, following Cameron's eyes. "Dana tried to clean it up but I guess it set in."

"Don't worry about it," he said.

Nate's wife Dana came in when she heard her name.

"Can we stay here beyond the two week spell?" she asked. The kids like this place a whole lot better than that shelter."

"Unfortunately I won't have enough room for the others if you go any longer than your spell. We're overloaded as it is, and remember," he said to Quinton, "no piano in the afternoon. Someone might hear you."

* * *

In between her talks with Ben, Kaitlyn found herself wandering the island campground. Malachi saw her sitting by the water and crouched down in the grass beside her.

"Great place to think," he said.

"What happened to Ben's son?"

Malachi plucked a blade of grass and squinted at her through the sunlight.

"That's not my story to tell."

"Just figured you'd know."

Malachi stared out at the water.

"Did you know this river leads straight to the ocean?"

"Why's he doing this?" Kaitlyn asked.

"Ben's been doing these weekends for as long as I can remember."

"No. I mean why's he so determined to make sure *I'm* okay? He could have pressed charges, or just let me off without giving me another thought."

"Let me ask *you* a question," Malachi said. "Is it really so bad having someone in your corner?"

"It's been my experience that no matter what they say, people are never really *in* your corner."

"Well Ben isn't most people. Better start thinking about making your way back for dinner soon."

"You really won't tell me about Ray?"

Malachi raised his eyebrows at her. He was surprised she knew Ray by name.

"You might not want to go tugging on that line, little minnow," he called out as he was leaving.

* * *

As Ben and Kaitlyn walked toward the chapel, the dirt road was spotted with light from the steeple between the shadows of the branches. When they stepped inside, Kaitlyn saw that Malachi and the rest of the team were sitting in the first two rows with the center carved out for her and Ben. The sanctuary was filled with stained glass windows, red cushioned chairs, and of course, hanging over the center of the stage, was the cross. It was dimly lit with rope lights that made it appear to be glowing. To the best of her recollection Kaitlyn had never been in a church before. She didn't know if the very design of the room was intended to evoke feelings of reverence but somehow it did. What was it she was supposed to gain from looking at the cross? Sadness? Hope? Wonder? She was surprised when she'd felt a surge of all of those things. Bill made his way between the pews and stood behind the podium ready to address everyone.

"This seems a bit formal," he said, and then walked out a few feet and took a seat on the stage instead.

"I noticed you were looking up at the cross when I came in," he said to Kaitlyn. "Do you have any questions?"

She shook her head.

"Okay then. I'll just tell you something you may or may not have heard before. God loves you Kaitlyn. Not because of anything you've done to deserve it, but because it is in his nature to love you."

She thought about that and weighed it against the life she'd had.

"I know Ben has become your guardian, so you've surely heard about Jesus."

She nodded.

"So, a lot of people know who Jesus *is*, but something they often don't realize is that, though the things he did, were for the sake of everyone, they were done very personally. Christ, for your sake, was born. Christ, for your sake, lived a sinless life, though he was tempted to sin. Christ, for your sake, took on your sin and died in your place. Christ, for your sake, rose from the dead. John 3:16 says that God gave his only son to die in our place. When I feel particularly hopeless, I like to insert my own name into that verse. I'd like you to think of it this way. For God so loved *Kaitlyn* that he gave his only son."

"If he's God, why couldn't he find some other way to do it?"

"You mean an easier way than allowing his son to die?"

"Yes."

"I won't pretend to know God's reasoning for that. I think the point is that he *didn't* take an easier way out. God demonstrated his love for us this way—while we were *yet* sinners, Christ died for us. People often forget that part and believe that they have to become someone worthy of love before he will love them. God doesn't operate that way."

"I need some time to think," she said.

"Of course," Bill said, nodding. "These things can be a little overwhelming at first."

Kaitlyn didn't feel overwhelmed. She believed everything Bill had said, but couldn't shake her anger at God for having given her a life that until recently felt more like a sentencing.

It was nice to have finally met you," Bill said, smiling. "Ben speaks very well of you."

She looked at Ben and furrowed her brow.

"Don't look so surprised Blythe," Ben said, grinning. "You're not all that bad."

* * *

Kaitlyn hovered above her notebook tapping her pencil against the desk. Ben had told her to write down all the words that wrongly described her, but she was finding it a grueling task. She reached for Ray's final journal instead. He had gone to jail for possession with intent to distribute and Ben had to bail him out. Ray refused to tell anyone that he had only been protecting Jason from a far worse fate, and that left Ben and Rosie to believe that he had become caught up in a world of buying, selling, and using drugs. Crushed by the loss of the respect of both of his parents, Ray planned to tell them the truth, but couldn't figure out how to do that without hurting his friend. Kaitlyn flipped through Ray's notebook trying to find some evidence that he had finally explained the situation, but the rest of the pages were blank.

She got up from the desk, wondering if Ben knew these things. Ray's journals had been buried in that trunk she found in his bedroom closet. The dust in his room made no secret of the fact that Ben hadn't been able to bring himself to go in there. He had asked her to stay out of that room and now a big part of her wished she had. She wandered down the hallway until she found herself on the men's side of the dormitory. She paused outside of Ben's room, afraid to knock. How could she tell him about Ray when he'd never even brought up the kid's name? She thought about turning back but she reasoned that whatever had happened to Ray, Ben had the right to know that he had been wrong about his son. That thought gave her the courage to reach out and knock. The door fell open, but Ben wasn't there. She turned to leave when something on his desk caught her eye. It was a letter addressed to John and Ellen Deckland. Ben hadn't yet slipped it into the envelope. Beside it were her report cards and a picture of her with Caesar and Roofus. She sat down and began reading.

> John and Ellen,
>
> I am filled with sorrow that you haven't yet returned any of my previous letters, but my unrelenting hope urges me to continue to write to you on Kaitlyn's behalf. My hope is that you will one day want to meet with her, to get to know her, as I have gotten to know her, and find the same qualities of strength, courage, and generosity that I have found. Not only would she be overjoyed to meet her brother Joshua, but I believe she would truly be an asset to his life. This young woman, who has been farmed out from one home to another for the whole of her life, has become a straight-A student, an avid reader, and one of the truest joys I've ever known. I don't want to push you, or be intrusive, but I feel I would be remiss if I didn't tell you both that you are simply missing out by refusing to even meet with her. I have enclosed her latest progress reports and a photo so you can see for yourselves that she poses no threat to you or your son.
>
> I remain, hopeful,
> Ben Gerard.

Kaitlyn put the letter back on the desk and wiped the tears from her cheeks. The lights from the steeple seared through the dormitory window beckoning her. She left the building and trudged down the dirt road, toward the church, lost in the weight of Ben's words. The cross, though seemingly radiant in the midst of the dark sanctuary, was no longer lit. She kneeled at the foot of the stage and considered all she'd learned that night. She closed her eyes and thought about how fortunate she was to have someone like Ben in her life. When she opened them, the cross was glowing. She looked over her shoulder and saw Lucius standing in the sound booth near the light panel.

"I'm not here to bother you Miss Katie, I just like it better all lit up."

Lucius rubbed the back of his neck and looked toward the door.

"You don't have to leave," she said. "I have no idea why I'm even here."

"Maybe you just needed to clear your head," he said in his soft voice.

"Yeah," she agreed. "Did you steal his bike too?" she asked.

Despite the size of him, she couldn't imagine it.

He nodded and looked her in the eyes.

"I was looking for a way out," he said. "I was going to drive it off a bridge, but Ben caught me and saved my life."

They sat together by the glowing light of the cross. She reached for his gigantic hand and held it.

14

Lost and Found

BEN LOOKED AROUND THE sanctuary, where the entire team waited for Bill to lead them in a morning service. He looked over at Malachi.

"She knows she's supposed to be here right?" Ben asked him.

"Yeah, I told her first thing this morning," Malachi said, shrugging his shoulders.

"I'm sorry," Ben said to Bill. "Maybe I should go check on her."

Bill motioned to the doors with his eyes. When Ben looked back, he saw Kaitlyn walking in with her sketchbook in her hands and Lucius in tow. Lucius nodded at him and took a seat in the last row.

"Everything okay?" Ben whispered, when she finally reached his pew.

She smiled at him through glassy eyes and continued making her way up to the front to address everyone.

"For God so loved the world he gave . . . " she said and stopped. Her shoulders fell and she looked up at Lucius.

"He *gave*," she repeated and stopped again. "My whole life I've been looking at all the things that were taken. My parents were taken. My little brother was taken. My home—my life was taken. Every time I turned around it seemed like something else was being taken away that should have been mine. Last night I spent some time with Lucius right here under this cross. He told me how much planning went into this weekend just for me. He said the whole team gathers in this chapel every night when I go to sleep just to pray for me. He told me how he lost his daughter . . . and how *you* lost *yours*," she said, looking at Rick. "He told me the only reason you two can go on living without those girls is because you have faith in a God who *gave* more than he took. He told me the reason I was supposed to write down all the things that have been *wrong*, was so I could nail them to this cross and try to make them *right*," she said, pointing to the smaller cross that had been wheeled in for later that morning.

"For God so loved *Kaitlyn*," she said, looking at Bill, "that he sent Ben her way. For God *so* loved Kaitlyn that he gave her a home and taught her to read. For God so loved Kaitlyn that he gave his *only* son and then made sure she found out about it. For God so loved Kaitlyn that he gave her the gift of faith to believe it."

She opened her sketchbook and ripped out a page.

"This is a place I have dreamed about since I was five," she said, holding up a sketch of the house where she always imagined her family might live.

She smiled at Lucius and he came forward then. He nodded at Ben and handed Kaitlyn a hammer and nail. She ripped the sketch from her book and handed the book off to Lucius. She climbed the steps to the smaller cross and nailed her sketch to it.

"I always thought this place represented the life that was taken from me and I've drawn this picture a hundred times—maybe trying to get it back. I don't know. Don't get me wrong; I don't want to burn it. I just think it's about time to let go of *supposed to* and start thinking about what *could be*. After all, the goal is to leave here without some of those wrong ideas I've been carrying around," she said, smiling at Ben.

Ben wiped his eyes and nodded at her.

"I couldn't nail to the cross what I wrote down last night, because what I wrote was the truth. *Lost and found* . . . that's me. For God so loved Kaitlyn, that when life lost her, he sent an entire search party to go and find her."

Bill stood up and nodded.

"I don't suppose you want to preach for me tomorrow morning," he said.

Rick made his way over to her. He pulled her into his chest and held her there as tears flowed from his eyes. He pushed her back a few inches and slipped a fishing hook around her neck.

"Welcome to the club," he whispered, kissing her forehead.

* * *

"I'll need you to plan an elegant but casual dinner for four," Angela said to the new maid, Georgia. "And don't forget to have the guesthouse ready for Mr. and Mrs. Stowe."

Cameron hurried down the stairs.

"Grandma and Grandpa are coming?" he asked, wide eyed. "When?"

"Tomorrow. You're white as a sheet."

"Why don't they stay in the main house this time?" he asked.

"Don't be ridiculous. They always stay in the guesthouse. That's why your father and I had it built," she said, walking away.

Cameron's heart was racing as he pulled out his phone. He dreaded asking for Bill's help, but he knew the humble pie he was about to eat, paled in comparison to letting Angela find his guests in the backyard.

* * *

"It looks as though your weekend will have to be cut short," Ben said to Kaitlyn. "It seems Bill will be here soon with a bus full of homeless people who need food and lodging. Malachi can take you home and I'll be there later."

She had wanted to talk with Ben about Ray's journals but now was clearly not the time for that.

"You'll need help. I'm not going anywhere," she said.

"I've learned that arguing with you is pointless—also there isn't time," he said, heading for the door. "How are you at making up beds?"

* * *

Bill pulled the bus on to the campground with twenty-eight refugees from the Stowe's guesthouse who would stay at camp for the length of their various spells from the shelter.

"Tell me about the boy," Ben said to Bill.

"Do you remember last year when you asked me to spend some time with the kid who'd just lost his father?"

"Rocky's nephew?" Ben asked with wide eyes. "The one who was causing his mother a handful of trouble?"

"Oh, he's an entirely different kind of handful now," Bill said, shaking his head.

"You turned him into a caped crusader," Ben said laughing.

"I wish it *were* funny."

"Well," Ben said, "he needs someone to pull back on the reigns, to be sure, but I seem to remember another kid who once had a savior complex . . . and I'd say *you* turned out okay."

* * *

"I'll take those," Michelle said.

Kaitlyn handed off the laundry basket and headed for another load in the washer.

"I can finish up," Michelle offered. "I think you've done enough."

Kaitlyn nodded.

"Long day?" Michelle asked.

"You could say that."

She surmised that Michelle was about the same age as she was. Kaitlyn recognized the same tinge of self-preservation on her she'd worn herself for most of her life.

"Have you met Nate and Dana?" Michelle asked.

"The couple with the kids, yeah," said Kaitlyn. "For some reason I thought you were with them."

"I am," said Michelle. "I mean, I've been traveling around with them for the past few months. They're not relatives or anything, just nice people."

"I figured they were too young to be your parents."

"Parents?" Michelle said, laughing, "Oh gosh no. I lost my parents years ago. I did have a crazy alcoholic grandmother—probably didn't even notice I left."

Kaitlyn found Michelle so light-hearted for a homeless kid, it was almost off-putting.

"So now you stick with Nate and Dana?"

"Dana's like the cool older sister I never had," Michelle said smiling. "Nate's another story."

"He seems really quiet," said Kaitlyn.

"He hardly ever says a word. He's having a really rough time with the loss of their son. Justin fell out of his second story bedroom window when he was three. Nate was supposed to be watching him when it happened and he can't forgive himself. After the accident, he got so depressed he lost his job, they lost their house—lost their whole life."

"That's not fair to the other kids," Kaitlyn pointed out. "They still need those things."

"The whole situation is a mess," Michelle sighed. "I felt sorry for myself because I had no shoes, till I met the man who had no feet."

Kaitlyn looked down at Michelle's sneakers and furrowed her brow.

"No," Michelle said, laughing. "It's just an expression. I mean, I always thought life dealt me a crap-hand until I met Nate and Dana. I've heard him wake up screaming from nightmares. He'll burst into tears at the sight of a little kid Justin's age. I've seen him stare into nothingness like he's in a coma at the mention of the kid's name. Losing your parents is rough," she added. "But losing your kid . . . well it's like a special kind of hell from what I can see."

"I guess I never thought about it that way," Kaitlyn said.

"Well, thanks so much for feeding us and doing our laundry. I'm guessing we'll be out of your hair soon," Michelle said, sighing.

As Kaitlyn watched Michelle carry the basket back to her dorm room , she felt almost paralyzed by the conversation. It occurred to her that she had been so wrapped up in her own pain, she'd failed to see the world around her. She wanted to tell Ben about Ray but now feared opening his wound. Perhaps the most considerate thing she could do, would be to simply leave well enough alone.

* * *

"Maybe we should think about telling Joshua sooner rather than later," John suggested, with Ben's letter in his hands.

"Maybe I should stop showing you these letters, so we can stick to our original plan," said Ellen.

"Well, even if we wait to tell him, *we* could at least meet her. I mean, look at this kid, she's not going to hurt anybody," he said, looking at Kaitlyn's picture.

"Absolutely out of the question. She still thinks of him as *Matthew Blythe*," she said, as though the name were poison. "Is that really a door you want to open, John?"

Joshua stood in the hallway outside of his parent's bedroom listening. *Who is Matthew Blythe?* he wondered.

* * *

"Thank you so much for all of your help the past couple of weeks Katie," said Olivia, as she sipped her tea. "Things should be returning to normal around here now."

148

"Well, this is better than sitting around waiting for Ben to get home from another fishing trip," Kaitlyn said, smiling at Iris. "At least I feel like I'm being useful."

"I suppose he goes out on those pretty often," said Olivia.

Kaitlyn nodded her head. She wondered if Ben's passion for putting on those weekends had something to do with Ray. She'd thought of a hundred different ways to lead Ben to stumble upon Ray's journals now that she'd put them all back inside the trunk in his closet.

"Hi Cameron," Olivia said, as he came around the corner into the backyard with Bill. "I don't know if you've met Katie yet."

They looked at each other for a moment.

"Dr. Livingston, I presume," Kaitlyn smirked.

He let out a bigger laugh than he'd realized and then caught himself.

"Bill, can you run Katie home?" Olivia asked. "She's been working in the dorms all evening . . . again."

"That's okay, Ben's expecting me to call for a ride any time now," said Kaitlyn.

"I can take her," Cameron said quickly. "I'm going that way."

"Which way would that *be*?" said Bill, restraining his laughter.

"Out . . . I guess," Cameron stammered.

Olivia raised her eyebrows, as if to ask Kaitlyn's permission and she nodded back, shrugging her shoulders.

She watched the trees rush by as they drove. Cameron kept pushing buttons until he found a radio station he liked. When he caught himself singing along, he stopped immediately, then turned it down low.

"You know they call you Robin Hood?" she said, eyeing him.

"I'm aware."

"Why were you hiding all those people at your house?"

"Because I had nowhere else to put them."

"Well, what happens to them when they leave the camp?"

Cameron sighed as though he carried the world on his shoulders, although he'd become delightfully distracted by Kaitlyn's presence in his car.

"Sorry I asked," she muttered, after his lengthy silence.

"They can go back to the shelter, but only for a limited time. They need a real solution," he said, slapping the steering wheel with the palms of his hands.

She was impressed by his determination to make a difference in their lives, though his passion seemed a bit mismanaged in her opinion.

"How did you get mixed up in all this?" she asked, as Cameron pulled into the driveway.

"Do you have time for a story?" he said, turning off the car.

She shrugged her shoulders and nodded.

* * *

"We should start looking at colleges soon," Ben said, scooping up some peas and dropping them onto his plate.

Kaitlyn lifted her head from her book and nodded.

"I've been thinking of dual enrollment to get a jump on my degree."

"What might you enjoy doing with your life?" he asked.

"Social work. There are far too many Blythes out there who think no one cares for them."

"In case I haven't said it lately, I'm very proud of you."

"You have," she said smiling. "But you can keep saying it . . . it just never gets old."

"Indeed."

"How many fish so far?" she asked.

"God always provides," he said sighing.

"Next time you go out fishing, can I come along?"

"I have told you a dozen times, these trips are no place for a young lady."

"Are you forgetting how we met?" she smirked.

"How could I ever forget that day?"

"I know you and Malachi think I'm this helpless little girl but I can handle myself."

"Not helpless . . . precious—which is why the answer is no."

* * *

Angela pulled her sleeves up and pushed the hair out of her face. She wondered if these people would hate her for having money, or worse, what if they robbed her? Where had Cameron put her purse? She couldn't remember just then. She flattened her palms against her pantsuit, hoping no one noticed how sweaty they'd become.

"Mom, here," Cameron said, snapping her from her anxious thoughts, as he handed her an apron and ladle.

She pulled the apron around her neck and managed a dry smile. Cameron chuckled to himself. He knew this was not what she'd had in mind when she offered to help.

"This is Henry," Cameron said, pointing. "Henry, this is my mother."

"Hello," said Angela, holding the ladle beside her face.

Cameron motioned to the food with his eyes and she began spooning mashed potatoes onto Henry's tray.

"You have a mighty fine son Ma'am," said Henry.

"I'm very proud of him," she answered, trying her best to avoid making eye contact.

"He's about the best friend a guy could have," he stammered, before making his way to a table with his tray.

She glanced at Henry's back and then forced a smile at the next person in line, who learned that she was Cameron's mother and explained that she didn't know what she would do without him. It seemed over the half the people Angela served that night had some story about his generosity and willingness to help. As she looked at him, where he leaned over the counter, speaking to everyone who passed, she couldn't help but see him for the first time. Not only had Cameron become a grown man, he'd become a man who was deeply admired. He looked over at his mother, wondering what she was thinking, and smiled at her.

After the kitchen had been closed down, Cameron found his mother out back with Bill and John.

"We were just telling Angela how much you'll be missed around here when you leave for Stanford in the fall," Bill said.

Cameron gulped down the remaining water in his bottle and nodded. He knew he should be excited to begin college but the fact that people at the shelter would be on the streets in his absence made him weary every time he thought about it.

"How many people would you say we could fit into the guesthouse without it becoming a fire hazard?" Angela asked, with a cunning smile.

Cameron furrowed his brows at her and shook his head.

"How on earth would I know a thing like *that*?"

"Well, how many people from the shelter have you *had* there at one time?" she asked, folding her arms.

"I assume someone told you I had people staying in the guesthouse," he said, looking over at Bill and John.

"Oh Cameron, how naïve do you think I am?" she said laughing. "When you moved the piano in front of the couch to hide that stain, the jig was pretty well up. Also, the gardener told me."

"Why don't you seem angry?"

"I was," she admitted. "I kept wracking my brain trying to figure out where I had gone wrong with you. Also you finally agreed to go to Stanford and I certainly didn't want to rock *that* boat."

Bill and John could see the conversation between them growing more personal and politely excused themselves, heading into John's office. Angela folded her arms and looked out at the city lights against the night sky.

"But then tonight—I don't know. I came here to see what had so captivated you—what had grabbed your attention in a way I never could."

"And?" he asked.

"And I realized, you're not mine. You never were."

He looked at her quizzically.

"You're my *son*, you always *will* be, but tonight I realized, a child is only yours on loan for a season, only yours for a moment. Your life has called you here, to these people. You belong to it . . . you belong to *them.*

"What are you saying . . . that I shouldn't go to Stanford?" he said with a note of excitement.

"No no no," she said, waving her hands. "I'm saying, just because *my* calling to help falls more along the lines of catered benefits, doesn't mean I can't lend a hand with *yours.*"

"Wait a minute," he said laughing. "Are you suggesting taking people in while I'm away at school?"

"In very controlled, limited numbers."

"What? Really? Mom, you would *do* that?" he asked, as his eyes glazed over with tears.

She smiled at him, feeling as though she'd just leapt from a moving train.

15

Miss Katie

CAMERON LOOKED IN THE rearview mirror at the bike on the trailer.

"Are you sure Ben will be gone all afternoon?" he said to Kaitlyn.

"How many times are you going to ask me that?"

"Well, last time he nearly caught us," Cameron pointed out. "Did you fasten the motorcycle down tight?"

"Yes Cameron, it's fine."

Once he parked, they unleashed the bike and went back down the road to sit in Ben's truck. Kaitlyn pulled out a deck of cards and shuffled them, then turned toward him and dealt them each a hand.

"Bill still keeping your volunteer hours to a minimum at the shelter?" she asked.

"I'm only allowed to help when I'm home on weekends until I graduate."

She looked over her hand and arranged her cards.

"You can't really blame him for being upset with you. Hiding all those people in your mother's guesthouse was pretty irresponsible," she said chuckling.

"Oh? Please continue the lecture as we wait for someone to steal Ben's bike, so we can chase them down the road."

"Fair enough. So, your mom really started taking people in when you left for Stanford?"

"A few."

"She doesn't seem the type."

"Tell me about it," Cameron muttered. "Anything on your brother?"

"Not yet," she sighed. "I keep sending letters though. Ben says it's just a matter of time."

"I'm sure he's right," Cameron agreed.

"Look," she said, pointing out the window.

A car slowed near the bike but then kept going.

"You're just trying to distract me," he said. "I won, your deal."

"So, Bill's right too you know," she said, dealing the cards again.

"About?"

"You'll do a ton more good for people after you've finished college."

"And where do they sleep and eat in the mean time?"

"You can't save the whole *world* Cameron."

"Said no future social worker . . . ever."

"There's something I've wanted to ask you about," she said eyeing him.

"Since when do you tip-toe around a subject?"

"You hang out with Bill pretty often when you're home, right?"

"Probably more than either of us would care to admit," he said, smirking as he examined his cards.

"All joking aside?"

"Okay," he said looking at her.

"How can you dedicate your life to making other people's lives better and *not* believe in God?"

"Who says I don't believe in God? I go to LWC all the time when I'm home."

"Come on Cam, this is *me* you're talking to."

"What is it you really want to know Kate?"

"You've become my best friend and I don't even know what you believe. Are you still an atheist?"

"I can't deny the validity of Christian history," he said. "Though a lot of my professors would disagree with that statement. I'm just not certain I'm sold on the idea of God as an explanation for all of creation."

"Then how do you propose we all got here?"

"Certainly you've heard of evolution," he smirked.

"If evolution is true what makes you think God wasn't behind it?" she asked with a smile.

"So, you believe in a God who created everything, but you don't believe he could do it in six days?"

"I never said that. I don't think any of us can begin to know the mind of God."

"You're starting to sound just like Bill."

"Cameron! The Bike! It's gone! Go!"

He tossed his cards and started up the road.

"There he goes!" Cameron yelled, pointing

"Could be a she," Kaitlyn said. "They're headed for the bridge. That's where I crashed the bike."

"Let's hope they drive better than you do."

"Says the guy who's fishtailing all over the road!" She yelled. "You forgot to disconnect the trailer!"

Kaitlyn turned to look out the back window. The trailer was lagging behind the truck with the open gate slamming up and down over the asphalt.

"Should I stop?"

"And let them steal the bike? Of course not!"

"I can't stay in the lane!"

Cameron swerved and hit the guardrail. He over-corrected and hit a tree. The truck had caved in on the passenger's side and stopped in the middle of the road. He looked over at Kaitlyn. She had a cut on her head and some blood dribbled down her face.

"Kate! Kate!" he yelled, trying to wake her.

He pushed open the driver's side door and fell onto the asphalt. Before he could pull her from the passenger side, a car came barreling around the curve and slammed into Ben's truck. He watched in horror as the trailer broke away and the truck rolled onto its roof and spun. Kaitlyn looked like a ragdoll getting tossed around the upside down truck, until it finally stopped spinning.

* * *

Ben walked into Kaitlyn's hospital room and stood at the foot of her bed. She looked so small, the bed seemed to swallow her up.

"Who would have ever thought a little bit of a thing like you could get herself into so much trouble?"

Her eyelashes fluttered and Ben got closer.

"Katie? Katie?"

Ben felt Malachi's hand on his shoulder and turned to him.

"How is she?" Malachi asked.

Ben motioned for the door so they could speak in private.

"It's not good Mal. She's sustained massive internal injuries and her body is shutting down. The doctor said there's a slight chance at best that she'll ever wake up."

"How did this happen?"

"She was trying to fish for the weekend."

"Why on earth would she attempt a thing like that?"

Ben squeezed his eyes shut and shook his head.

* * *

It seemed all Ben did now was pray. The Consuming Fire boys took round the clock shifts sitting at the hospital with him. No one dared utter Ray's name, but the thorn in Ben's side was throbbing more than ever and Malachi feared what losing Kaitlyn might do to him.

Cameron read to her from one of his favorite books. He licked at the cut above his lip. The metallic, bloody taste was a bitter and painful reminder that while his wounds continued to heal, she lay in her bed, barely alive. He put the book down when Ben came into her room and he looked at him with pleading eyes.

"I'm so sorry this happened," Cameron said, choking back his tears.

"What on earth would possess you to do something so stupid?"

"I tried to tell her that it might be dangerous, but she wouldn't listen," he cried.

"What exactly were you planning to do if you'd caught that thief?"

"I suppose neither of us really expected it would go that far. We'd been fishing before and no one ever took the bike."

"She trusted you Cameron, and look at where it got her!" Ben yelled.

In reality, he was talking to himself then. Cameron was simply an easy outlet. Ben should have guessed she'd pull something like this when she'd asked to go fishing so many times.

Lucius saw Cameron sobbing at Kaitlyn's bedside and came in. He put one hand on Cameron's shoulder and put his other hand out to stop Ben from saying anything more.

"I believe he heard you, Mr. Ben," Lucius whispered. "We all did."

Ben looked at Cameron, shook his head in disgust, and walked out.

Cameron buried his head in his hands and Lucius patted him on his back, sharing the kid's pain.

"Suppose we don't know if he's done with her yet."

Cameron didn't know what Lucius meant but lacked the inclination to ask.

"I've been learning that sometimes God sends people our way just to let us know he's listening. Miss Katie is one of those people."

Cameron looked up at Lucius then.

"I asked him to show me if I was the right one to be telling folks his story. Because of my size and my past, I thought no one would ever be able to hear me—I was thinking all they'd see is a big scary criminal. Miss Katie showed up in the chapel right in the middle of that prayer—figured that couldn't be a coincidence. Just like the first time I prayed and he sent Mr. Ben. God sent *this* little messenger to tell me he was calling me, just like I thought he was," Lucius said, brushing her tiny hand with his. "I think God sent her to give Mr. Ben a message too."

"What kind of message?" Cameron asked.

"Same message he sent her to give to *you*," Lucius whispered, as his eyes burrowed into Cameron's.

* * *

"Staring at the elevator isn't gonna bring them here any faster," Malachi said, handing Ben a cup of coffee.

"The plane landed over an hour ago. What's taking them so long?" Ben asked, waving the cup away.

He perked his head up when the elevator doors opened but sank bank down into his chair when two nurses got off and headed into the intensive care unit.

"They'll be here," Malachi assured him. "They said they would come."

"Yeah . . . now that she's *dying*," Ben snorted. "It had to come to this for them to act like human beings. What'd she ever do to them Mal? Nothing—that's what," Ben said standing. "All she wanted was a home!"

Malachi stood and put his hands on his friend's shoulders.

"You're making people uncomfortable," he said. He raised his eyebrows and looked into Ben's eyes. "The nurses are gonna kick us both out of here."

Ben looked at the nurses, who were now staring at them from their station. He took the coffee cup from Malachi and sat back down.

"I don't know what I'll do if they're too late. All she wanted was to meet her brother Mal and I couldn't even give her *that*."

As Malachi searched for words of comfort and encouragement, John and Ellen Deckland emerged from the elevator with their son.

"Thank the Lord," Ben gasped.

"I want to see my sister," Joshua said to Ben, shaking loose from his mother's grasp.

Ben hurried to her room with Joshua in tow.

"Kaitlyn. Kaitlyn," he said a bit more sternly. "Someone wants to meet you."

Joshua looked at Ben with the same green eyes and turned up nose Kaitlyn had.

"Go on son," Ben said to him. "Don't be afraid."

Joshua looked her up and down, not quite able to believe she was his sister. He had only found the letters a few days before Ben called offering to fly them all out to her bedside. At only thirteen he tried to digest the situation as it unfolded before him.

* * *

"So you're Kaitlyn's *real* parents?" Frankie asked.

Rick nudged him in an attempt to quiet him.

"No. I'm John, and this is my wife, Ellen," he said, shaking hands with Frankie, Rick, Malachi and Lucius. "We adopted Joshua when he was a baby. He's Kaitlyn's natural brother."

"Why didn't you adopt *both* kids?" Frankie asked frowning, and Rick bumped him harder this time.

When Ellen broke down into sobs, John put an arm around her and let her cry.

"I'm just glad you agreed to bring him," said Malachi. "I know Ben's real thankful for that."

"When Joshua found the letters he was furious with us for not telling him that he was adopted—and even more so for not telling him he has a sister," said John, still holding his wife.

"We thought we were doing the right thing," she cried. "Now he's going to lose her and he'll never forgive us."

John pulled her closer and kissed her temple.

"I'm not sure *I'll* ever forgive us either," he murmured against her.

* * *

"Mr. Gerard?" said a soft gentle voice. He looked up to see the bluest eyes and sweetest smile he could ever recall seeing in a hospital.

"Yes Ma'am?"

"Hi. I'm Maureen. I understand you're Kaitlyn's guardian?"

Ben nodded.

"Let's talk a little bit about her condition ok?"

"Of course."

"Is it okay to talk here? Or would you prefer we speak privately?"

Ben looked around at everyone and nodded.

"It's okay, we're all family."

"So, what's going on is that Kaitlyn has gone into multi-system organ failure."

"But her brain is still functioning?"

"Yes," said Maureen, cautious not to give him false hope. "Soon, she'll be transferred to my floor. That's the palliative care unit."

"Palliative?"

"Let me explain a little bit about what that means."

Ben knew exactly what that meant. Rosie went to the same floor before she faded away. He was stupefied that the word now pertained to his little minnow.

"Her body is still in agony from the accident. So much so that she can't wake up, even to say goodbye, unless we manage her pain. Even then there's no guarantee that she'll wake up," said Maureen.

Ben tried to wrap his head around what she was saying.

"So, the hope is that you'll medicate her out of her pain, so that she can wake up long enough to say goodbye?"

Maureen's eyes filled at the thought that she had to tell this man his little treasure was going to die.

"Yes. I'm so sorry."

"How long?" he asked, as tears rolled down his face.

"I can't say," said Maureen. "I would stay close by."

She touched his arm then and looked deeply into his eyes.

"If she wakes up, even for a moment, say everything you need to say."

* * *

It took a full day of medication before Kaitlyn's body responded, and when it did, Ben was right beside her. He had just about fallen asleep holding the guardrail on her bed when he felt her hand tighten around his arm. He jolted awake and looked her up and down as though he hadn't seen her in a hundred years.

"Can't move my legs," she said, not recognizing her own voice.

"They're broken," he whispered, with tears streaming his face.

"Did Cameron catch the fish?" she asked, raising her eyebrows.

"Let's not worry about that now," Ben said, narrowing his gaze on her.

She studied the look on his face.

"I'm not okay, am I?"

"Now don't go saying things like that," he said, smiling through his tears.

"Since when haven't we been straight with each other?"

He shook his head. He couldn't bear to tell her she was dying.

"Guess that explains why I feel like this."

"Like what? Are you in pain? Should I call the nurse?"

"No—it's just that my body is telling me the things you're afraid to say."

She closed her eyes and Ben remembered what Maureen told him about time being of the essence.

"I need to bring someone in to see you," he said quickly. "Please don't go back to sleep yet. Please."

"Ben wait," she whispered, holding on to his arm. "I can't stay awake for much longer, I need to ask you something."

"Trust me, this can't wait," he said.

She squeezed his arm again and shook her head. He narrowed his brow at her, realizing he should listen to what she had to say.

"Where's Ray?" she asked.

"What?" he asked. "Ray? My *son* Ray?"

"Please tell me."

"Now is really not the time for this," he said, heading for the door.

"Please."

Ben shook his head and searched his mind for the quickest explanation possible.

"I killed him."

She opened her eyes and stared at him in disbelief.

"He was robbing the house. I thought he was an intruder and I shot him by mistake."

"Did you ever make up with him?" she asked.

"Make up?"

"After you bailed him out of jail, did you ever speak again?"

He wondered how on earth she knew about any of this and set aside his anger for whomever had told her. He'd deal with them later.

"Did you?" she pursued.

"The last time I saw Ray, he was robbing my house. It was dark. I shot him and he died in my living room. We never made up. We never got him the help he needed for his addiction. My ache for my son is so awful—it's why I started Consuming Fire," he finally confessed.

He began to sob and reached for her hand. "Now it looks like that very thing will cost you your life."

"Ray was never a drug addict," she whispered, behind closed eyes.

"I assure you, he was."

"No Ben," she said, opening her eyes. "The trunk . . . in his room. Read his journals. They'll explain everything."

Ben's eyes widened and he shook his head.

"He was just like you," she whispered smiling. "He only took your things to help his friend."

She wouldn't let go of his arm. She pulled herself up to look at him.

"You taught me to read, and I read his story. You never . . . lost . . . Ray."

Her arm went limp and she fell back against the bed as one of the machines began making an awful sound. Maureen came running and Ben got out of her, way though still reeling from their conversation.

* * *

"Is she?" Ben asked, when Maureen finally came out to the waiting area.

"No, but she's exhausted. That was likely the last time she'll speak."

When Ben broke down crying, Maureen held him in her arms.

"Goodbye is such an important part of the journey," she said in her soft voice.

"She was the answer to all those prayers," Ben cried. "God sent that little minnow right into me at the river that day, so I'd be sure to catch her."

Maureen had no idea what he'd meant by that so she just let him talk. Soon everyone in the waiting room knew the story that Ben had been guarding so closely.

"All these years I thought my son died for nothing—a meaningless, horrible death that I caused," he sobbed. "We couldn't understand why a kid like that would just turn—he just turned. Rosie was heartsick, I'm sure it's what killed her."

He turned to Malachi then and held out his hands.

"Did you know Katie was reading Ray's journals?"

Malachi shook his head. He didn't even know Ray. All Malachi knew about Ray was what he had read in the paper and what Ben had told him, which was very little.

"Ray wasn't lost . . . he *wasn't* lost," Ben cried. "I never would have known that, if God hadn't sent Katie to me and now she's going to die."

Cameron looked over at Lucius. As Ben pieced together Ray's story, Cameron thought about the things Lucius had said, and wondered if Kaitlyn really *was* some kind of messenger.

"Isn't there anything you people can do?" Frankie yelled. "For crying out loud, she's just a kid!"

Rick put his arm around him and nodded.

Maureen thought it best to try to explain it further.

"Because the accident hurt Kaitlyn's liver, her kidney's have begun to shut down. She's going into what is known as Hepatorenal Syndrome."

"And there's no cure for that?" Frankie asked.

"Yes. A liver transplant."

"Ok, why didn't you tell us that to begin with?" Ben asked smiling. "So we just need to get her a liver."

"Even if we put her on the list for transplant, the odds of our finding a matching donor before she passes are about zero."

"So our only hope of saving her is if someone who's a match dies right now—as in *today*?" Cameron asked.

"Well, if she had a living relative who was a match we could do a partial transplant—but I understand she's adopted," Maureen said, looking at Ben. "I'm sorry, we're just out of time."

The entire waiting room fell silent and Frankie looked over at Ellen. She shook her head, but before she could say anything her son stood up.

"Joshie no!" Ellen cried.

"I'm Matthew Blythe. My sister can have *my* liver," he said.

Ben stared at the boy. It was an awful lot to ask of a thirteen-year-old, but what choice did they have?

"You're her biological brother?" Maureen said. "I don't understand."

"Might that save her?" Ben asked.

"It could," Maureen said nodding.

They all looked at John and Ellen.

"Can we have time to think about this?" John asked

"She's about out of time," Maureen said.

"I'm not afraid—I'm doing this," Joshua proclaimed.

Maureen looked at his parents, realizing this must be a long and complicated story.

"I can take him right now to be tested."

"I know you all think we're being selfish," said Ellen, "but Joshua is our only child. We can't *have* children of our own. If something happens to him—well, he's all we have."

"This is for you and your husband to decide," said Maureen, "but you should know that your son is very likely Kaitlyn's only hope."

Joshua stood in front of his parents with his hands stuffed in his pockets.

"I just found out I'm not really your son. You weren't even going to tell me for who knows how long. My real parents are dead. I'm not going to let my sister die too."

Ben was amazed at the similarities between him and Kaitlyn as he silently prayed that they would listen.

John looked him in the eyes and realized it was only the first of many adult decisions his son would make. John nodded and Joshua turned to Maureen.

"Hurry," she said, "we have to do this now!"

As they raced down the hallway and out of sight, Ellen fell weeping into John's arms.

"You're doing the right thing," Frankie said. "You don't know Katie, but if the situation was reversed, she wouldn't think twice about saving your son. Imagine if *he* was the one laying in a hospital bed about to die and she showed up out of nowhere. Wouldn't you pray that she would help him?"

Ellen stopped crying and raised her head from John's shoulder.

"Yes . . . I would," she whispered.

16

Any Given Day

THE SUN MADE ITS way across the horizon and Ben stirred his iced tea with his straw. He caught Kaitlyn's eyes from across the table and smiled at her.

Cameron stood up and tapped his glass with his fork, calling everyone to attention.

"We nodded off during your last toast," Bill called out laughing.

"Be that as it may," he said, smirking at Bill, "Kate and I would like to thank you all for being here today to celebrate the opening of our newest shelter. May everyone who needs it, find solace at the, Raymond Gerard house of refuge," he said, lifting his glass.

In the whole scheme of things, Ben Gerard would have said he was right where he should be. Of course he'd have said that on any given day.

The end